Requiem

History of Sol Book 3

Steven Dutch, Chris Masterton

Masterton Dutch Multimedia

History of Sol

Book 3: Second Edition

WRITTEN BY

Steven Dutch & Chris Masterton

EDITED BY

'Mick'

COVER ART BY

Jason Giraldo

COVER DESIGN AND FORMATTING BY

Chris Masterton

Acknowledgements

Since starting out on this journey a number of years ago, we have met some really awesome people. The biggest influence of all has been a bloke called Mick, who reached out to us with a helping hand after we released the first edition of this story. We are better writers because of his patience, feedback, and attention to detail.

Massive thanks go to Jason for another fantastic cover, helping bring out visions to life, and to Amanda for help with formatting. Shout out to Marie (for bringing the snacks) and Amanda for being great company at the conferences.

Like most authors, we have some very understanding partners, Rach and Yani, who accept that we need to be glued to our computer screens for hours on end and are always there for emotional support.

Finally, all the fans who have read, enjoyed, and even loved our books; thank you for coming to meet us at the conventions, giving us feedback, and for supporting our journey!

DATAFILE

Enceladus

NODE 1

Description: Enceladus is the sixth largest Moon of Saturn and is a major hub for the Saturn Alliance Colonies. It is home to thirteen mining cities built on the surface inside expansive bio-domes that sustain conditions required for human life. The colony is one of the largest producers of water and hydrocarbons, as well as various critical resources.

DATAFILE

The Saturn Alliance - Luume Colony

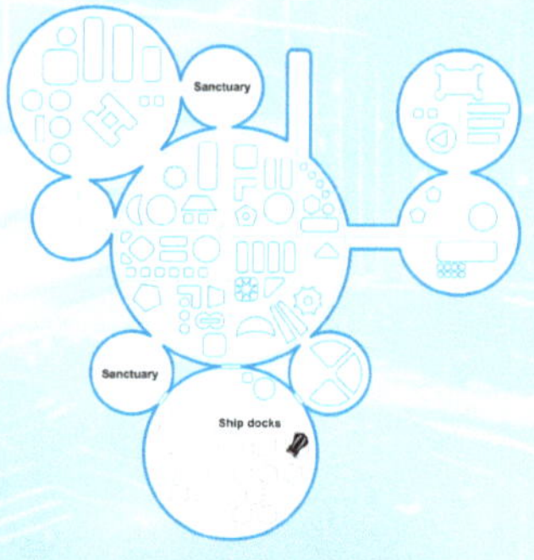

Luume is the eighth city constructed on the Saturn moon and comprises nine bio-domes extruding from the surface with passages, structures and mines extending for kiltrons underground.

The surface of the city is vibrant and teeming with life. Vegetation thrives due to the abundance of water from the Hydro Centre. Plants are cultivated in the sanctuary and moved into the city.

The lower reaches of the city are far less prestigious, with several sub-floors of metal passageways and mining stations leading deep underground.

CHAPTER ONE

Rendezvous

Diputs inspected his reflection staring back at him through the mirrored interface. He meticulously combed his hair and neatened his uniform.

"Mirror off."

The mirror vanished, replaced with a view of the tree-like structures of the Orlanna Spaceport. The sight was a welcome one. It was a chance to break free of the tiny crew cabin allotted to him and explore a new place he had never been before. Diputs was not claustrophobic, but he still tried to spend as little time as possible in his cabin. Making port was always a good chance to get out and soak up local culture. The sanitation compartment was but one half of his designated space. Just two steps backwards would take him across to his vertical bed against the far wall. Thanks to the suspension fields, it was no different to sleeping lying down.

A downward glance reminded him that he had somewhere important to be. The holographic text still hovered over his Link on the edge of the vanity.

'REPORT TO THE DC, IMMEDIATELY!'

Without further hesitation, he made his way through the winding corridors to a maglift, which carried him up twelve decks to the Operations floor.

He stopped at the door. He took a deep breath, straightened his uniform once again and pressed on the interface. There was no immediate answer. After a few seconds, the door vanished, and a view of the Delivery Coordinator's private office made it apparent: this wasn't a casual meeting.

Diputs' superior—Delivery Coordinator Jaynen Clark—wore his usual look of dissatisfaction. His red and grey Martian uniform was immaculate. He sat at his workstation facing the door, looking directly at Diputs. Someone was next to him, standing bolt upright as if at attention. Her brown wavy hair was tied back, and her uniform was dirty and worn out. She wore standard-issue Technician's overalls and a utility belt packed with tools. Despite her firm facial expression, her eyes showed fear. She looked uncomfortable.

Diputs entertained a slight smile, hoping to ease the tension. "You wanted to see me, Sir?"

Jaynen flicked open specs of the cargo ship on the holographic interface in front of him. "Come and take a seat, Diputs."

Diputs sat in the single chair opposite Jaynen. He glanced at the Technician, but she remained at attention.

Jaynen sat back in his chair. "You haven't been assigned to the *Epsilon* for long, Diputs. Yet, in the three runs since you have been the Operator, we have had more technical issues than in the last two Cycles!"

Diputs nodded slowly, wondering where this was going. "It's not my fault this old rig has a few cracks in it," he said jovially. When neither of their expressions eased, he continued. "Regardless, I still managed to get us to our destination, safe and sound. Ahead of schedule, I might add."

"Your reckless and foolhardy navigation has burned out three primary thrusters just getting us across the belt!" The bold accusation came from the Technician. "This isn't a racing ship, it's a cargo vessel," she added coldly.

"Listen, lady. I'm here to operate this ship, I know what it is and what it isn't capable of. It's your job to keep it going, not to tell me how to fly." Diputs watched the Technician turn visibly red.

Jaynen raised a hand to quash her growing outrage. "Look, Diputs, my job is to manage the delivery schedule. As such, I make sure there is enough time to get from one place to another *without* blowing an engine. Operating this ship and getting us about is not that hard. So when I have Technicians constantly complaining to me that they have to work double shifts to keep us going, you can see why I have to step in and do something about the situation."

"Of course, you're just doing your job," Diputs conceded. "I'm sorry I pushed the engines so hard. I won't do it again." He looked between the DC and the Technician. "Well? Can I go now?"

"I'm afraid it's not that simple," Jaynen said. He glanced at the Technician. "Serena and her team are struggling to keep up with the repairs that your actions have caused. You may have gotten us here a rotation early, but it will take twice that to fix the damaged thrusters."

"Doesn't the Station have people who can help?" Diputs suggested.

"This is a Saturn Alliance outpost," Jaynen reminded him. "They might be friendly with us at the moment, but I'm not about to just stroll in there and start asking for favours. Besides, I think it will be a much better lesson if *you* were to help with the repairs."

"But I don't know anything about fixing engines."

"Don't worry, I'll show you," Serena said. She finally let out a small satisfied smile. Diputs couldn't help smiling back. For the first time, he actually noticed her. Eyes like precious gemstones, her full lips and freckled cheeks. He realised he was staring.

"Diputs!" Raynor's voice crashed into his mind like a clap of thunder.

Diputs' eyes shot open and the reality of Rob's laboratory came rushing back. He removed the memory isolator from his temple, and shook his head, getting back to reality.

"We're here," Raynor said. "Get ready."

They had arrived on Enceladus.

DATAFILE

Memory Isolator

Robert Crane - Device Catalogue: Invention #473g

During my extensive research into the memory centre of the human brain, I was able to use a sonic beam to isolate specific memories stored there. Then, feed the information directly into the perception cortex to play the memory back as if it were really happening.

The device works exceedingly well. However, I think it requires additional consideration of the morality of its use. The first thing that springs to mind is personal use. To recall loved ones lost and even to regain missing pieces of information that lay dormant in our subconscious.

The second is that it may be used by the Enforcers to prove innocence or guilt in an alleged crime. This would mean that someone else would be experiencing another person's private memories. This is where it gets a little concerning. It opens up the door to the idea of stealing memories or implanting someone with false or stolen memories. What would stop someone from abusing this power?

In addition, I've not had the benefit of being able to study any long-term effects it may have on the individual using it, how it may alter their brain patterns and, how it may change their understanding and interpretation of what is real.

I have decided to keep this device in Beta, rather than turning it over to the Martian Space Science Institute, until I can ponder on some of these questions.

CHAPTER TWO

Requiem - C1099 S5 R15

An artificial breeze blew lightly through the foliage lining the outside perimeter of the Sanctuary of Life. Diputs looked around at the serene beauty of the tall trees and green grass laid out immaculately in front of him. He took a step off of *Galaxy's* access ramp and led his crewmates through the entwining paths, over a bridge and towards the centre of the garden where a large congregation had formed. Many wore white robes with purple trim over their clothing. He wondered if they held any significance.

The gathering briefly glanced at the procession, their gaze shifting to the stasis tube carried between them, and Serena's body within. She looked peaceful, lying there in the glass coffin with her hands clasped across her lap. Appel had done an excellent job at covering up the fatal wound and arranging Serena's body to look as though she were only sleeping.

Diputs was surprised by the size of the gathering. Serena had disconnected with everyone from her life in the Colonies; he had thought he would be the only one here for her Dispersion. He spotted her parents close to the altar. Their expressions darkened as he approached. He was surprised by the clear hate in their eyes as they watched him. It bothered him that their anger seemed to outweigh their grief.

They eased the tube into position and a mechanism in the altar slid Serena's body out of the glass. The tube retracted discreetly from view, leaving Serena lying unobstructed on the altar. One by one, people approached her and placed flowers over her body.

The altar began to glow as the Dispersion began. The flowers floated up above Serena and tiny orbs of light began rising with them, emanating from her body. Soon, she was entirely engulfed with light as every molecule in her body dispersed upwards and outwards, spreading throughout the garden.

Diputs reached up to try and touch the last remnants of his lost love. He allowed himself to shed a tear and found that more than one stung his eyes.

Serena was gone now. Her remains vitalising the vegetation which grew throughout the garden. Quiet conversation arose as the Dispersion concluded.

Diputs spotted Serena's parents again. They were still glowering at him. Were they angry at him for choosing to be away from Serena all those cycles ago? Did they hate him because he was not one of *them*? Or maybe, they were just sore that he was the last person to see her alive. Diputs had questions of his own; he wanted to find out why she was sent to sabotage the *M1 Space Station*, so he made his way over to them. Their expressions didn't ease as he approached. Diputs considered offering his hand but decided against it. "I'm sorry for your—"

"Save it, murderer!" Avilen said. Her lip trembled despite her harsh words.

Diputs couldn't help but notice how much Serena had looked like her mother. Especially when fired up like this. Avilen had barely aged in comparison with Resden, who was grey and frail from illness.

"Murderer?! You think *I* had anything to do with this?"

"You were with her when she was killed," Resden said. "What did you do to help her? Why were you even interfering?"

"I... I didn't..." Diputs' gaze darted between the two, wondering how this was suddenly his fault.

"Exactly. You didn't do anything to help her," Resden said. "You let her die."

"And prevented her from completing the will of the Divine," Avilen added.

"I couldn't... It all happened so fast."

"What were you even doing there?" Avilen asked. "You had no right to interfere with her mission."

"*You* sent her on the mission, right?" Diputs said.

"The Divine sent her," Resden said defensively.

Avilen hushed Resden and tugged on his arm.

Diputs didn't care if he made a scene. "Oh, so that makes it all alright then? Do you know what your *Divine* sent her to do? They were going to kill millions of people." Including him and his friends, he wanted to say. But Diputs was certain that little fact would be of no significance to them. "They were sent on a suicide mission. They were never going to make it off the station alive."

"No." Avilen shook her head. "They had a plan. They would have survived."

"That's what they thought, too. It was all a lie. The plan was never to make it off alive. Your leaders probably wanted to make martyrs out of them. But believe me, she died because of whatever it is you have gotten yourselves into here."

"But, because of you, she died for nothing," Resden said quietly.

They both just stared at him. The fire in their eyes had dimmed, their faces had gone blank and expressionless. It was obvious to Diputs that they had no further will to discuss the matter with him.

"You wanna hate me? That's fine. But it doesn't change the fact that you sent her to her death. Your faith has distorted your minds! She is gone and blaming me is *NOT* going to bring her back. You're lucky I don't turn you all over to the Enforcers right here and now, at your own daughter's Dispersion."

"Does that help you ease your pain?" The voice came from behind him. "Attacking a mourning mother and father at their weakest moment? What gives you the right to condemn them?"

"Condemn them? I'm doing nothing of the sort. *They* are the ones who…" Diputs spun to confront the stranger, but the fire he had felt was quelled by how old and frail the speaker appeared. Diputs looked around. Their heated conversation had drawn a crowd. He avoided their disapproving eyes.

The stranger inspected Diputs closely. "Ah, you are a splitting image of your father." He scratched the grey tuft of spiky hair on his chin. Diputs was stunned. He couldn't remember his parents. They had died when he was very young.

"I'm afraid you have mistaken me for someone else," Diputs said, hoping to avoid the whole topic.

"I don't think I have."

"And who are you anyway?"

"My name is Victr Evon. I am the Divine Cleric of Vassal D'Sol."

"The what?"

"Divine Cleric," Resden interrupted. "Why are you telling this heretic who we are?"

"Because this heretic is going to help us."

"Like he helped Serena?"

Evon reached into his robes.

"Wait just a minute here. I am not helping any of you do…" The words died on Diputs' lips at the sight of the compact firearm. He had no time to react, Evon was behind him, the muzzle pressed against his back. The other robed people pushed everyone back, forming a tight ring around them. Diputs' eyes darted frantically. He saw Raynor and Persephone on the fringe of the crowd. They had drawn their own weapons and were edging towards the hostile situation.

"I wouldn't do that if I were you," Evon said.

Diputs felt cold, his palms clammed up and he felt like there was a knot in his stomach. His heart raced, but he didn't want to do anything stupid to provoke this attacker.

"Just put the weapon down," Raynor called. "I'm sure we can settle this without needing to resort to violence."

"Of course we can. All *you* need to do is put *your* weapons down. Let us take our hostage and go. I promise if you don't follow us, I won't blow his brains out the side of his skull."

"Now, don't be so brash," Raynor said cautiously. "If you blow his brains out there will be nothing to stop us turning you into plant mulch."

"But that's where you're wrong, you see. My followers will never let me come to harm. *I* am the voice of the Divine. Any of them would gladly put themselves in harm's way so that I may live on."

Instantly, people enclosed on Raynor and Persephone, obscuring Diputs' view of them. A hand grasped his hair and jerked his head back. He felt a sharp sting on his neck, then Evon stepped away.

"It's time to choose, Diputs. Follow me or die." Evon walked away from him, the pain in his neck spread rapidly. The agony was crippling. He dropped to one knee and grasped his throbbing head.

"You are bio-tethered to me now, Diputs. If you don't follow me the pain will quickly kill you."

Diputs struggled to his feet. Evon took two steps closer to him and the pain eased.

"See?"

He stepped towards Evon and found himself trying to keep pace as they left the Sanctuary. The pain began to ease with each reluctant step he gained on Evon. He turned to see if he could get one last glimpse of his crewmates, but they were too busy scuffling with the crowd.

He followed Evon out of the Sanctuary to an uncertain fate.

DATAFILE

Dispersion

NODE 1

Dispersion is the process the human body is commonly subjected to after death as a method of disposal. It is also commonly used to describe the entire ceremony attended by family, friends and associates to farewell the deceased.

NODE 2

Using the Slovinsky Method, the matter which makes up the human body is converted back into Adaptive Bioenergy, which is scattered throughout the garden and used as nutrients to extend the life of the vegetation in the Sanctuary.

NODE 6

It has been proven that exposure to the Bioenergy created as a result of the Dispersion will (in minute amounts) affect people, as well as plants. It has been observed that people who work in the Sanctuary and are exposed to a lifetime of Bioenergy often live on average up to 3.8% longer than people in similar industries.

It is also noted, but not proven, that in some instances, people will feel 'in better health' for a short time after exposure to such energy.

CHAPTER THREE

Underground

Diputs vanished into the crowd of people standing between Raynor and his target. Raynor holstered his weapon and pushed violently at the people standing in his path, but they did not budge. They were too densely packed together. He thought that wearing such robes was somewhat out of place. Of course, so was abducting people.

They were completely surrounded. Persephone kept the crowd at bay with a firm grip on her blaster. She spun around and people retreated as the muzzle swung towards them. Raynor lurched forward and grabbed one of the attendees by the collar and threw him to the ground.

"Where are they going? Where is your leader taking him?"

The follower only stared dumbly. Raynor raised his fist, but the man didn't flinch.

"Raynor!" Persephone shouted.

"What?!" He lowered his fist and released his grip. The man fell backwards and scurried away with the rest of the crowd, who were fleeing in all directions like a swarm of insects buzzing away, back to their hive. Only a scattering of people still remained.

Lazarus approached them. He was talking frantically into his Link. Raynor could hear Rob's voice demanding to know what was going on.

"Are we just going to let them all get away?" Persephone asked.

"No, just wait," Raynor instructed. "Laz. Tell Rob to track us with Red's scanners. Go back to the ship and wait for us." He turned back to Persephone. "Seph, time to hunt."

They watched the last robed follower run towards the Sanctuary exit. Raynor gave chase and Persephone followed close behind. The exit to the Sanctuary led into a series of cold grey corridors, twisting and turning down into the rocky surface like tree roots burrowing into the ground. He quickly lost sight of him and had to slow to listen for the faint scratching of boots on metal. They stepped lightly through the well-lit service passages, occasionally stopping to be sure they could still hear movement ahead. Whoever they followed kept a jogging pace, without care of the sounds they made, which echoed through the underground maze.

A ramp lead down to a level where smooth stone encased them. Coloured pipes ran in all directions, the occasional doorway littered the otherwise plain walls. It was darker in the lower levels. They had now clearly left the city and lost their target. They slowed their pace, hoping for some indication of where to go. The silence was broken by the tell-tale clunk of a metal hatch being opened. They moved quickly and quietly in the direction of the sound and halted at an intersection in the passageways to peer cautiously around the corner. Raynor saw a panel being secured back into place on the far wall and silently signalled for Persephone to follow him. Raynor cautiously placed his ear to the metal pane. It was quiet. He pulled at the edges of the panel, wincing at the loud clunk as it gave way. Behind it was a vertical shaft cut directly into the rock, with a ladder leading down into the darkness. Raynor let Persephone go first, then grabbed a rung with one hand, carefully replaced the panel behind them with the other, and proceeded carefully down the shaft.

The further they went down, the colder it got. Raynor shivered in the darkness and wondered how deep this pit went. There was no light in the shaft, only the sense of touch and sound to guide them down the ladder. When they finally reached the bottom, Raynor estimated that it had only taken them a couple of levels down. He felt loose rocks crunching under his feet as he carefully stepped away from the ladder. He listened for any sounds that would give their target away, but all was still and silent. They had completely lost all sign of the man they were hunting. Raynor activated a light on his wrist, it illuminated a tunnel that slanted down from the ladder.

"Well this is creepy," Persephone said, her voice echoing down the tunnel. "Five hundred cycles since they built these, and they still haven't got any lights down here."

"Shh," Raynor said quietly. "The mines underneath Luume go on for kiltrons. Many of these have been abandoned for a long time, but sooner or later we should come across a mining station or an abandoned checkpoint. It wouldn't be hard to get lost down here and never find a way out."

"Look over there, the footsteps in the dust. The tracks just vanish."

"A hover car? Down here?"

"These outlaws are a bigger threat than anyone realises," Persephone said. "If we don't stop them, we're going to have another Mars Riot on our hands."

They walked in silence for some time as they ventured down the empty tunnel. After a while they came to a large cavern. There was a metal structure—a circular building built in the centre of the cavern. Mining equipment was strewn all about, and tunnels branched out in various directions.

"Great, we lost him," Persephone said.

Raynor pointed his light towards the building. It was two levels high but didn't reach anywhere near the top of the jagged cave. No lights shone from the large windows. A one-person hover-rover was parked in front of a wide, open doorway.

"Maybe not," Raynor replied. He headed towards the building.

As he got close, he noticed the two large hangar doors set in the far side of the cave wall. One of them bore the Saturn Alliance sigil. They stopped at the sound of metal against metal. A whine filled the cavern, the sound of a motor spooling up. As they looked about for the source, the ground trembled and the gigantic doors begun to grind open. Raynor and Persephone sprinted for cover in the abandoned building, dimly lit by emergency lighting. Raynor switched off his light and let his eyes adjust. He quickly assessed the room for suitable cover among the dusty machines and equipment covered with draping fabric. He wondered if the man they had followed also sought refuge in here. Raynor spotted stairs leading up to the second level. He looked over at Persephone and pointed up the stairway. They stalked quickly and quietly up to the next level while staying as low as possible.

The slow drone stopped, and he heard voices. He peered out of a glassless window and saw a patrol of six people in dark grey body armour moving through the giant doors. They were well armed. Each of them carried a not so standard range of Atlas tech. From particle beam rifles to a hypervelocity railgun. It was the sort of weaponry that special-ops units carried. Guns like that would come with headgear that included enhanced motion detection, lowlight acu-vision and an audio targeting system. Raynor did not want to pick a fight with them.

They spread out and shone lights around the spacious cavern.

"Ops, this is Recon Three. The north-east entrance looks clear, are you sure the sensors detected multiple instances?"

Over the comms a voice crackled. "We've got friendly inbounds coming from all directions. Just make sure none of them have been followed."

"Got it."

Persephone pushed herself up from her crouch position to peer down on the group. "What is such a heavily armed unit doing down here?"

"Could be the same as us, but it sounds like they are guarding whatever is behind those doors," Raynor whispered back.

"What was that?" One of the soldiers exclaimed, looking straight in the direction of Raynor and Persephone.

Raynor hoped the soldier couldn't see him in the relative darkness of the building and motioned to Persephone to be silent.

One of the soldiers flipped his visor down. "Your imagination. I've got nothing on visuals."

The squad strode up to the building. One took a closer look at the hover-rover. "This vehicle has been moved, recently."

"Of course it has. We use it all the time. You're just being paranoid."

Another inspected the front of the building. His gaze drifted over the window Raynor and Persephone were secretly watching through; they cautiously crept back, deeper into the shadows.

"There are a couple of hidden passages around here, too. We should check the building just to be safe."

"Why don't we just level it?"

One of the soldiers shoved his teammate. "Don't be so blighting lazy. Just get on with it, check the building. We have other tunnels to get to."

Raynor listened to half of the patrol scuffling around on the ground level, while the other hung back, keeping a casual watch over the cavern. He heard footsteps coming up the stairs to the second level. Slowly and cautiously, someone was coming up the stairs to find and kill them. Raynor made eye contact with Persephone. She already had her small handheld electrolaser pointed at the top of the stairs. He did the same, thought he didn't think they would be very effective against that level of body armour.

He focused on keeping his breathing steady while he stared down the short barrel of his blaster. Unlike the laser, Raynor's weapon would hopefully do enough damage to the stairwell to collapse part of the structure, leaving them with very few options to escape. He could see the faint silhouette emerging from the floor at the top of the stairs.

"Found it!" The muffled voice came from beneath them.

"What?"

"A hidden tunnel. Help me seal it up, would you?"

Raynor quietly exhaled as the shadow of the figure retreated down the stairs. The hissing of a plasma torch echoed through the building, followed by several long screeches as something heavy was likely dragged over the top of it.

"What's taking so long in there?"

"Just securing the building. Everything seems to be clear."

The giant doors screeched and groaned once again as the soldiers retreated into the secured complex.

"Now what are we going to do?" Persephone whispered. "Even if we could get in, there will be a lot more of *them* inside."

Raynor straightened and ran his hand through his hair. "It doesn't seem logical that the robed guy would lead us down here, ditch the rover and then walk back up another tunnel. He came down here specifically to enter that compound, and he must have known about the hidden entrance."

"But does that mean those guys were all with the outlaws?"

"Those weren't just any regular Saturn Alliance Enforcers. Whatever is going on down here, we need to get in contact with the others and see if *Galaxy's* scanners can find another entrance. Red would have tracked our Links."

"Well my Link has no signal, so I guess we are going to have to head back up anyway," Persephone said.

"That's unusual. They should still be working fine, even this far underground." Raynor activated his Link. He scowled as the 'no connection' tone sounded. "Mine's down too. That can't be a coincidence. Let's get out of here, before we run into any more of these soldiers."

Raynor and Persephone had managed to get all the way back to the hangar through winding underground passages. They trudged slowly across the expanse of landing pads back to *Galaxy*. It had been a long walk. The access ramp was still extended, inviting them aboard. Up the ramp was the sterile sheen of polished metal and white lights.

"Where the fuck have you been?" Lisa said as she strode towards them with purpose across *Galaxy's* lobby. "I've reported the abduction to the Enforcers. No one had any idea what happened to you or Persephone. We couldn't even locate your Links."

Raynor didn't want to tell her where he and Persephone had been, or why they were untraceable for so long. If he told her, she would surely report the location to the Enforcers.

"We were looking for Diputs," Raynor said.

"So? Where is he?"

"We lost them in the underground tunnels."

"That's it? You *lost* him? How is that useful information?"

"How is reporting it to the Enforcers useful? They are practically soldiers, not detectives. If they knew who Diputs was with they would probably kill the lot of them. Including Diputs!"

"It doesn't matter what you think the Enforcers will do. We are in another colony. We must follow the correct procedure. If we just go off on some vigilante mission to rescue Diputs in this political climate, it could start a war!"

Raynor realised he needed to cast doubt on the Saturn Alliance. Make it look like this wasn't just the work of outlaws. Then, as a Martian Observer, she would have no choice but to look into it herself.

"I never said anything about *we*," Raynor said. "Persephone and I followed one of them underground. He led us down an abandoned mine where we encountered a well-armed patrol that seemed to be protecting something down there. I think the Saturn Alliance are hiding something."

"Are you saying the Saturn Alliance abducted Diputs?" Lisa said with a laugh.

"Who else?"

"Outlaws," Lisa suggested. "I asked Red to playback the Dispersion for me. I saw the abduction!"

"What if the Saturn Alliance are just making it look like another outlaw attack?""To what end?"

"I don't know!" Raynor shouted, throwing his arms up in the air. "Maybe they don't want to tribute a third of their forces to the UAE."

"Your argument is trivial. We know Serena was an outlaw. Her and her people infiltrated the Lunar Colony and tried to kill millions of people. These people at her Dispersion were the same people who sent her. That means they are outlaws!"

"Or, that the Saturn Alliance was behind the attack on Lunar," Raynor continued. "And, they're hardly blending in when they dress like that out in public. They are clearly making some sort of statement."

Raynor watched her face while he let that sink in. Her stern expression didn't change.

"What could the Saturn Alliance possibly want with Diputs?" Lisa asked.

"Maybe he figured it out, and it was the only way to silence him." Raynor walked over to a large interface on the wall. "Red, bring up a map of the mine shafts and overlay it with a trace of our Links whilst we were down there." The tabletop glowed, the hazy light coalescing into a spaghetti tangle of intertwined tunnels above it. "See this area, here." Raynor pointed at a blank space on the map. "Both ours and Diputs' Links lead towards it. Then they just disappear."

"That doesn't mean Diputs is still down there. They could have destroyed or discarded his Link at some point, perhaps even left him for dead somewhere. But if there really is a secret operation going on down there, then I wouldn't be a very good Observer if I didn't attempt to assess it to find out if the Saturn Alliance could be a threat."

Raynor smiled, "I'm going with you. If Diputs is in there, we need to get him out."

"That's just fine with me," Lisa agreed. "I'm going to need you to show me how to get down there anyway."

"Getting down there isn't the problem," Raynor said. "The reason we came back to *Galaxy* was to try and find a way in. The place seems to be well guarded. The patrol mentioned various hidden entrances scattered throughout the mines. They sealed one, but I'm sure we can find more."

"If it can't be scanned, what are we going to do?" Persephone asked.

"Leave that to me," Lisa said. "Get your gear together and meet me back here in one hour."

DATAFILE

Vassal D'Sol

WARNING: Threat level Beta

Advice: Terminate on contact

NODE 1

Meaning: 'Servants of the sun'

The Vassal D'Sol is a dangerous outlaw sect of religious fanatics who worship the light of the sun.

It is alleged that they believe the light speaks to them (through their leader), controls their actions and gives them supernatural powers.

NODE 4

History & Leadership: The group is controlled by an individual named Victr Evon, who goes by the title 'Divine Cleric'.

Evon was born on the Saturn Alliance moon; Rhea, C984 S24 R5, where he was assigned the role of Extraction Supervisor in the Angorian mines.

At some point it is believed he came into contact with a group of idealists, who taught him how to manipulate people, and Evon began to recruit followers.

Evon's Value was abrogated when he abandoned his role and fled to the wastelands of the Kuiper Belt to join the outlaws, though his devout followers remained (in hiding) and used his teachings to grow their ranks in anticipation of his return.

It is alleged that the Vassal D'Sol may have been involved with the destruction of the M1 Orbital Space Station.

CHAPTER FOUR

The Chosen One

Diputs felt cold. He opened his eyes to utter blackness and his head pounded to the beat of a drum as he tried to remember how he had gotten here. He felt his thoughts slip away like sand through open hands. He must have been drugged. Images and sounds of Serena's Dispersion flashed through his mind, causing his stomach to tense and fill with sadness. He could hear someone outside. Muffled talking. A woman's voice. Then the door hissed open. His eyes burned as the room lit up. He covered his face with one arm and lowered it slowly as his eyes adjusted.

The familiar face of Serena's sister, Romea, looked down on him. She looked a lot like Serena, but with softer features. Her skin was smooth and lacked the weathering of age. She smiled and offered him a tube of Organix. "Drink this. It will help you feel better."

"Where am I?"

"We are underground." She sat on the bed next to him and felt his forehead.

Diputs sipped at the Organix and assessed the room. It was bare, but for a few amenities; a simple bed with fitted sheets, a chair in the corner, and a workstation with an interface displaying the

Saturn Alliance sigil. Romea was still inspecting him. Her clothing was the same as everyone else at the dispersion.

"So, what's with the robes?"

"Oh, these?" she stood abruptly and spun around. The robes crisscrossed around her; white cloth wrapped around her crimson suit, holding it snugly to her slender body. "We normally only wear them down here where we aren't seen, but the Divine Cleric said that it won't matter for much longer. That's why we wore them to my sister's Requiem. It was a show of defiance."

"Probably not a very smart one," Diputs added.

"The authorities don't know we're down here. They are too busy worrying about the other Colonies. They are convinced that there will be another war."

"You mean the one your sister was trying to ignite?"

Romea crossed her arms. "There is a much bigger plan. It's not our place to question it."

"That plan, whatever it is, is going to get a lot of people killed. And I sincerely hope that you're not one of them!"

Their eyes met. She stared at him until a mischievous smile broke out to mask her sadness.

"I have one for you, too." She pulled him up to his feet. The room spun momentarily, but he managed to stay upright. She placed the robes over his head before he could protest and pulled it down over his Martian uniform.

"What? No. I look like an idiot."

"You look fine," she said patting down the fabric at his waist. "It will help you fit in."

They were now standing intimately close to each other.

"Why was I brought here?" he asked bluntly.

She looked up at him with deep blue eyes. "I don't really know. You made quite a scene at my sister's Requiem. I…"

"I'm sorry about your sister," Diputs said. "Please understand I didn't mean for any of this to happen."

"Serena died in the service of the Divine. She will live on in the Light for all eternity. That is all anyone can ever hope for."

"So, you truly believe all this garbage?" Diputs asked with disappointment.

"We have been shown the truth that the Colonies have been suppressing for generations. Divine Cleric Evon has freed us from their control. We are all servants of Sol now."

"You don't look very free. Hiding underground, dressed in these freaky robes. What exactly do you do down here? Plot the destruction of society while mass murdering as many people as possible?"

"We do no such thing! We are all part of a greater plan. One which you have set back immeasurably." She took a deep shuddering breath. "You will have to atone for that in some way."

"*Atone?* Well how exactly do you expect me to do that?"

Romea sat on the bed, looked at her hands, then met his gaze. "We are building weapons, right under the colonies' noses'. They think we are building the weapons for them, but they have no idea that we control the entire operation. We are going to defeat the Saturn Alliance. I want you to join us!"

Diputs said nothing.

"Don't you want to be on the winning side? On *my* side?" she pressed.

He sat down next to her. "I don't want to be on any side. I just want to get away from here! If there is a war coming, then neither of us should be a part of it. I was there when Serena died. I watched a high-speed round penetrate her helmet and…"

Romea consoled Diputs, lightly rubbing his back. "She knew what she was getting into and she knew the risks. She died fighting for a cause she believed in. We all believe in it and would willingly die to serve the Divine." Her eyes displayed the same determination that Serena had when she spoke to him about her convictions.

Diputs knew there was little chance he would convince Romea to change her mind. But he had to try. "And what did her dying achieve? What did she accomplish by giving her life for this ridiculous cause? There is no need for you to die here fighting for some made-up story. You could come with me. I have a ship. We could escape here together and get far away from this madness."

Romea turned away from him. She shook her head slowly and wiped her face on her robe.

"My sister was murdered by the Colonies. You watched her die and yet, all you want to do is run back to them?"

"I want to live! I didn't do enough to stop them from killing Serena, I know that. I don't know what I could have done, but I know that I didn't do enough. I can't just stand by and watch the Colonies murder you and your parents as well."

"So you will just stay a slave to them? If you want to save us, then join us. You are smart, Diputs. You could lead us and save us from the Colonies."

"No, I can't."

Romea stood up and neatened her robe. "Well, then. I can't go with you." She went to leave but paused in the open doorway. "She didn't deserve you." The door hissed shut behind her. Diputs rubbed his chin while he contemplated that.

He patted down his clothing in search of his Link, but it was gone. His headache had eased, so he decided to explore his new prison. He tried to access the workstation, but it was locked. He started knocking on the walls to try and determine how dense they were but could only hear the dull thud of solid stone. He turned over the bed, sending the mattress and sheets sprawling. Nothing underneath. He made a lot of noise ripping apart the room, but no one had come to see what was going on. He turned his attention to the interface panel beside the door. This room was a living space, not a containment cell. There must be a manual door release somewhere in the case of an emergency. The locking mechanism was controlled by a small interface panel beside the door. He tried to pull it off the wall with his fingers, but it wouldn't budge. He looked around for anything he could use, went over to the bed and picked up the metal frame. It was lighter than he expected, so he hurled it towards the workstation. The interface shattered into jagged pieces. He grabbed a shard and wrapped it in some bed cloth, then used it to pry the door panel away from the wall. Behind it was the manual switch to release the door lock. He flipped it and then went to work pulling the sliding door open.

He peered out and then cautiously sidled through the doorway and into the adjacent room. This area was larger than the bedroom, with a table large enough to sit ten people, a plush lounge and an Organix dispensary over at the far wall. Six doors enclosed the room with no distinguishing features. One by one he checked them by tapping on each adjacent interface, only to see them flash red. The second to last one was unlocked, so he stepped out into the stone corridor.

Sconces lined the walls, holding glowing orbs that cast a warm light on the polished smooth shades of brown and black. They gleamed like a continuous sculpture. He stopped to listen for anyone coming, but there was only silence, so he pressed on through the endless winding corridors. He gathered he was still on Enceladus, most likely deep underground. But how far from Luume, he could not know. He found an interface that displayed an internal layout of the complex and tried to figure out where he should go. He needed to find out what these people wanted with him and, if possible, convince Serena's family to leave with him before they got hurt.

He had not heard the two shadowy figures who were ghosting down the corridors. But for all their stealth, they made no effort to be completely invisible. Nor did they increase their pace to intercept him when he hurried off in the other direction. He looked over his shoulder periodically as he wound through the long passageways. The robed figures followed but did not attempt to close the gap.

Finally, he reached the entrance to a grand amphitheatre. In the centre of the room was a single beam of light emanating from the ceiling, shining down on a raised circular dais. Someone was floating in the light, at least a metron off the ground, arms stretched out and head tilted back looking directly up at the source.

The two shadow figures startled Diputs as they grabbed him by the arms and ushered him down the incline towards the dais. They had pulled back their hoods since entering and Diputs could now see their faces. They were young men, both with short brown hair and faint stubble on their faces. Each of them garbed in the same robes as Romea had been. They were slightly taller than Diputs and held him with a firm grip. As they got closer to the light, Diputs recognised Evon, the one who had abducted him. Diputs tensed his muscles and tried not to go any further, but the guards easily dragged him closer, up the steps surrounding the dais.

"In the light, we see all," Evon's voice boomed. "In the light, we know all. In the light, all is pure." He descended, arms still outstretched, as if he were welcoming Diputs.

"Is that supposed to impress me?" Diputs asked. "Why have you brought me here?"

"This," Evon said, looking up at the ceiling. "Is the pure light of Sol. It is focused down from the surface and magnified to invoke its Divine presence."

"Why?"

"We serve the Light of the Divine, Diputs. Only the truly worthy can even bear its touch."

"Is that so?" Diputs asked.

"Allow me to demonstrate." Evon looked to one of the guards who were standing back from the dais. "Brenton, place your hand in the light."

"But, your worthiness—"

"Do it! I command you."

The guard reluctantly placed his hand in the light. At first, nothing happened. He looked at Evon.

"Go on," Evon said.

Moments later, the hand began to smoke. Agony gripped the guard's face as his skin seared and blistered, burning in the intense light. He screamed out in pain, pulled his hand away and looked at it with horror.

"Go and get yourself treated," Evon said. "Euron, go with him. I will be safe alone with Diputs."

"But how..." Diputs asked.

"How do I not get burned? I have been chosen by the Divine Light to lead these people. My purpose is to bring peace and righteousness back to Sol. To cleanse it of the evil."

"So, what do you want with me?"

Evon had drifted down to touch the floor. He left the light and crossed the room to a water station where he poured himself a drink. "We had a plan, Diputs. Carefully constructed and meticulously executed. We have built solid foundations in each colony with which to undermine the rule of evil. Everything was in place, after so many cycles of careful manipulation and then... you. You ruined it. I don't know how, but somehow you were there, and you corrupted Serena and ruined the mission."

"*You're* responsible for killing Serena," Diputs said angrily. "You put her there. You made her do those things."

"I am but a vessel for the will of the Divine. Serena would never have jeopardized the mission. Unless—"

"I still don't understand," Diputs interrupted. "Why do all of this? What did you hope to gain by destroying *M1* and the people on it?

The Colonies would still exist, the Nexus would go on. They would assign new Representatives and Peacekeepers and you would be right back where you started."

"But there would be chaos, for a time. Chaos which we could use to fan the embers of hatred and turn them into the flames of war. The Colonies would each react with aggression. Crushing each other until..." Evon fell silent for a moment. "We would sweep in with superior force and release the survivors from the tyranny of the Colonies' rule. People could choose to do as they like, believe what they want."

"As long as they believe and do what you tell them? What makes you any different? At least in the Colonies we have order and purpose. All you bring is chaos and death."

"Freedom is a frightening thing," Evon explained. "The unknown of a future where you are not told what to do and what to think by your leaders. But it is a future everyone deserves and all who serve the Light will get. Unfortunately, the ultimate price we must pay is in blood. What makes us different is we care about something bigger than ruling humanity. We care about the souls of the people who sacrifice themselves for the cause, whether intentionally or not. The pain and suffering of those who die in the process is only temporary. If they are pure of heart and soul they will return to the Light and be one with life itself, forever."

Diputs stood in silence, trying to make sense of all he had just learned.

"There is something special about you, Diputs. Serena sensed it. She always did have a wonderful connection with the Divine.

I believe you can help us. I knew it from the moment I first recognised you."

"Help you? Why in the depths of space would I want to help you?"

"The Divine has shown you to me. I knew your parents. They died to protect you, betrayed by those whom they loved."

"How could you know of my parents? I never even knew them."

"I know many things. Just like I know *you're not stupid*, Adran."

Diputs' heart thundered in his chest. He knew little of his childhood or his parents. But one thing he did know was his true name. His mentor, Barron Addler, had always told him to keep it a secret. That when the time was right, it would wield great power, but also great danger.

"Who were my parents? How do you know of them?"

"I grew up in the Colonies. I was like you once, I did what I was told without question, but I always knew that there was more to life than being a meaningless cog in the big machine. When I found out that I wasn't alone in feeling that way, I sought out others. *That* is how I knew your parents. No one hated the Colonies more than them."

"They were outlaws?"

"By colony definition, yes. But they were so much more! Help us and I will help you come to know the Light of the Divine, to know your parents."

Diputs' mind was spinning. He didn't know how to react or how he could even help. He didn't want to help Evon, but he owed it to Serena to help her family. If there was even the slightest chance that Evon could help him to know more about his parents, he had to take it.

"With the Colonies as strong as ever, I fear we cannot stay here much longer. Especially now. As far as anyone knows this is an abandoned mine. Only some higher-ups in the Saturn Alliance council know about this operation—and they certainly don't know who we are or what we are really doing."

"What *do* you do here?" Diputs asked, expecting another convoluted answer.

"For some time now, the Saturn Alliance has been expecting a war between colonies. This facility was setup to develop new weaponry and a fleet of ships to use against their enemies. It provided the perfect setting for us to infiltrate the operation and use the weapons for ourselves."

"What was that thing you did to me, back in the Sanctuary? That thing that made me follow you."

Evon smirked. "That is what we call a Bio-Tether. It locks you to another person. If you don't stay within a certain proximity of them, you feel great pain. But if you stray too far from them, you die."

"But I don't feel anything now."

"No. I have released you from its grasp. I believe you will stay for your own reasons. We need you to help us leave this place. Serena's family needs you!"

"Leave? Where are you going?"

"Far beyond the reaches of the Colonies. At the edge of the Kuiper belt, on a celestial body also made from ice, is a place for people like us. A place where we can be open with our beliefs and be free."

"Sounds magical," Diputs said facetiously. "So why don't you just stay out there? Why even fight the Colonies at all?"

"It is the will of the Divine," Evon said with certainty. "We need to save humanity from itself."

Diputs rolled his eyes. He was starting to think that the man saw no reason at all, that nothing could dissuade him from his ideas about the Colonies. "Don't you have ships?"

"Yes," Evon said.

"So, what is stopping you from taking them and leaving?"

Evon didn't answer right away. "Our Fighters won't carry everyone. But that's not all; there are some that think we should fight to the death, even if we fail to do any real damage."

"And you think I can change their minds?"

"Yes!" Evon took off his necklace. There was an amulet of a golden sun with a large yellow jewel in the centre. He placed it over Diputs' shoulders. "You were born to be a great leader, Adran—"

"Don't call me that."

"People aren't going to follow *'Diputs'*. You need to convince them that your parents live on in you. Live up to their legacy. Come with us to Neptune and you will get the answers you seek. All of them." Evon walked away from Diputs, leaving him alone on the Dais. "Walk free about the complex as you will. But I trust you shall not leave. Not without the things you desire."

Evon left, so Diputs turned his attention to the beam of light in front of him and toyed with the idea of grandeur that Evon had put into his head. If he truly was special, if he was born to lead these people, could he resist the Light of the Divine? Cautiously he ventured his hand out towards the intense light. He could see the specs of dust dancing gracefully in it. It didn't look so harmful. Mesmerized by its influence, Diputs reached out and dipped his hand in. He felt it drenched in warmth. An exhilaration ran through him and to his surprise, his hand didn't burn. There was no smoke, no searing pain, just a feeling of warm sunlight. He pulled his hand back abruptly. Could all of this have been just a trick? Maybe the guard had used chemicals to simulate the light burning him. Or maybe, just maybe, there was some truth in what Evon had said to him.

Maybe he *was* the chosen one.

DATAFILE

Bio-Tether

NODE 1

An experimental prototype weapon developed on the Saturn Alliance's Luume underground research facility.

The purpose of the device is to induce a state of bio-quantum-entanglement with the user's DNA.

A molecular sample is taken by the device, giving the controller the ability to inflict crippling pain or even death on the victim without needing to be near them. There is also a proximity setting, which allows the controller the ability to set a range limit the victim cannot stray past.

It is worth noting here that this technology is in direct violation of the Nexus Peace Treaty Section 189, with regards to the ethical treatment of diplomatic prisoners.

NODE 2

The only way to remove the Tether is to destroy the controller device (which may also result in death) or to remove the encoding from it, requiring an encryption key. This encryption key can also be bio-locked to a specific user.

CHAPTER FIVE

Infiltration

Raynor floated in his habitat, naked, back to back with Persephone. He held a small round silver device in his hands. Rob called it the 'Star', which was short for something. He had no idea what the letters stood for, only that it could transport him a great distance in the blink of an eye. It had allowed Lisa and Jake to escape with him from the outlaw battleship *Pywayrah*. And in that moment, he'd felt connected to them in a way that he could not express in words. After he had first used the Star, Rob told the Colonies that the rare element powering it was spent and the device burned out, which was a lie. So Raynor was determined to keep it secret, lest Lisa try to hand it over for the Colonies to weaponise.

He knew he could not save Diputs with this alone. There were too many unknowns; the size, internal layout, how many people were inside, where they would be keeping Diputs. He needed far more intel to formulate a viable plan. He didn't even know for sure that Diputs would still be in there.

"So, what's your plan?" Persephone asked.

"You heard; Lisa said leave it to her, whatever that means."

"And you're going to?" She laughed. "We both know that's not how you do things."

"She's an Observer," he reminded her. "She's supposed to be good at this kind of thing."

There was a ringing chime. His Link floated within reach, so he grabbed it and turned off the alarm.

"Well, hour is up," Raynor said. "I need to meet Lisa."

Persephone shifted against him, rotating to face his back so she could wrap her arms around his chest. He felt the press of her bare breasts on his back.

"I want you to hang back, for now," Raynor said.

"What?" she said incredulously. "You need me to watch your back. Especially with that cyborg around. She is unpredictable. We have no idea whether she is ever genuinely trying to help us."

"I know. That's why I want you to trail us. If we get in trouble, you can't help us if you're caught up in it too."

"Okay then." She sighed and rested her head against his shoulder.

In the lobby, Lisa was already waiting for them. Her usual silver skinsuit was replaced with black overalls and a tactical vest. Her dark hair was tied back. Raynor and Persephone had likewise ditched their Martian uniforms for plain unmarked jackets and trousers.

"Persephone, I didn't realise you would be joining us," Lisa said.

"Oh, I'm not. Raynor and I just like to dress the same," Persephone said.

"Persephone is going to float around the area and keep an eye out for anything suspicious. Apart from us," Raynor added.

"Suit yourself. Put these on." She handed him a pair of black boots and headed down the access ramp.

Raynor changed into the boots and then followed. "So, do you mind telling me how exactly we are going to do this? We don't even know what we are walking into here."

"That's what I am hoping to discover. Back on Mars, there is a central repository that has the plans and blueprints of every single space station, building and ship in the colony. The Saturn Alliance will have a similar database. I should be able to hack into it and find out where we need to go and how to get in."

Raynor stopped at the base of the ramp and looked up at the ship looming over them. "What makes you think it will be that easy to just *hack in* and find the blueprints to their secret base?"

"I never said it would be easy. That's why I need your help. I need to get admittance to a primary data node with direct access to this colony's internal Nexus. From there I can do the rest, but I'll be exposed and potentially vulnerable while I bypass their security measures and find what we need from a vast amount of encrypted data."

"So where do you suppose we find one of these primary data nodes?"

"Just follow me and listen to my instructions."

They followed; but there was only silence as they walked through the ship docks, which berthed all sizes of landing craft on its expansive deck. Automated cargo racks whizzed past them as they followed the clearly marked walking paths to the enviro-scanners.

Once they were cleared of any environmental contaminants that could be harmful to the ecosystem, they were granted access to the largest of the nine immense domes that made up the busy mining city of Luume.

Raynor looked up at the hundreds of reinforced triangular glass panels forming the structure overhead that protected them from the steamy atmosphere beyond. It was night outside, but the city operated on full brightness all rotation. Tall buildings filled the dome but were separated by recreational areas, including gardens and water features. The green of the city surface was far removed from the dirty filth of mining equipment and industrial machines deep underground.

"I'm going to hang back now," Persephone said. Raynor nodded and then followed Lisa into the bustling foot traffic.

Raynor looked over at Lisa, walking beside him. She seemed focused; instead of marvelling at their surroundings. Her head and eyes remained fixed straight ahead and she walked briskly with purpose.

"Have you been here before?" Raynor asked casually.

"No. You?"

Raynor laughed. "I have been to most places."

Another awkward silence followed.

"Why are you doing this?" he asked. "Why do you still fly with us? Surely you know by now we aren't doing any illegal experiments.

That was all Reen. What exactly does Swift think we are doing that warrants this level of observation?"

She scowled at the mention of Swift. Raynor was intrigued by this apparent tension between her and the Supreme Commander.

"I'm not here to discuss my orders with you, Raynor. I gave you a chance in the beginning to comply with my investigation and you chose to fight me every step of the way. Since I have been on *Galaxy*, I have faced the possibility of death on two occasions..."

"And yet, you're *still* here."

"What's your point?"

"After all that has happened to you. After Swift left you on *Galaxy* like a discarded pet. After he was prepared to sacrifice you on *Pywayrah* and the *M1 Space Station*."

"Wait. On *M1*? What did Swift—"

"Rob told me that he was about to blow the station up rather than risk it crashing into the surface of Lunar," Raynor said. "Clarissa talked him out of it."

"It would have been the right thing to do," she said without heart.

"Even still. How can you be so loyal to him?"

"That's none of your..."

He stopped and put his hand on her chin to turn her face towards him.

"Don't," she warned him bitterly.

He looked into her eyes, but she refused to meet his. She brushed his hand away and shook her head free. But it lacked her usual vicious fury. She was vulnerable.

A thought pressed him. It was more like a memory which he'd never had. Something left over from their time connected by starlight. Raynor cracked a smile. "Fuck me. You love him, don't you?"

"Of course not," she said. "That's absurd."

"Does he know?" Raynor laughed. He saw a flash of anger, but Lisa turned and walked away.

Raynor almost pitied her. He used this new information to reshuffle earlier events in his mind. The time Swift assigned her to *Galaxy* to watch over them. Raynor remembered her look of dismay when she had retracted her armoured helmet. Swift was trying to get rid of her.

Raynor wanted to press this advantage, not to hurt Lisa, but to turn her against Swift. He sped up his pace to catch up with her and she spun around to face him. This time, she looked enraged.

"You think you are so clever, Raynor. But you don't know me. You don't know what I have been through or what I feel. Mark my words, I *will* catch you doing the wrong thing. Swift tried to re-assign me, but I stayed because *I* want to be the one who brings you down. I'm not doing this for Swift, I'm doing it for *me*!"

Raynor ran his fingers through his hair. "Are you finished?"

Lisa stared back at him, a smug expression to mask her radiating fury. "Do you know what happened to Reen?"

Raynor shook his head slowly.

Lisa continued. "There are some people who cannot be rehabilitated, you know. What should we do with such people? If people like you were allowed to mingle with other Valueless outlaws, there is no telling what influence they might gain. People such as Rob; they know things about the Colonies that could be used against us." She poked him forcefully in the chest. "You and your crew are all far too dangerous to be allowed a second chance. Just like Reen. So they froze him. Suspended indefinitely in time. Not dead, but no longer a threat to humanity."

The threat was clear and it chilled Raynor to his bones. He considered for a moment, the irony that freezing Reen was a violation of the Nexus treaty, as punishment for Reen violating the very same treaty.

"*We* don't threaten the colonies."

"Not right now. Not yet. I won't let you." With that she turned and led the way into a wide entranceway of a towering building near the centre of the dome city.

The spacious foyer was mostly empty. The floor and ceiling flowed with a matching grid pattern of white squares, making the ceiling feel lower than it really was. A robotoid scanned them and the panel above their heads flashed red.

"This is the city's Central Athenaeum. You will have to hand over your weapon," Lisa said.

Raynor unclipped his holster and went to a counter beside the concierge desk. An administrator took it silently, flicking a receipt to his Link. Annoyance at Lisa failing to warn him competed with annoyance at his own failure to expect it. He noticed that she didn't have anything to hand over. He pocketed his Link as she joined him, and together they headed for the lift lobby. "High security for a data centre, isn't it?"

"They don't let outsiders in, normally. I had to alter your Link to give off a Saturn Alliance frequency."

"I had no idea you could even do that," he said.

She grinned. "That's not all I can do."

They stepped into a lift which took them up several floors. The doors opened onto a spacious dome with rows upon rows of holographic interfaces stepping up as they circled the room. In the centre was an enormous spherical holographic data matrix that flexed and moved slowly as it processed zettabytes of data. Hundreds of people either moved about the open space or were transfixed to an interface.

"You wanna hack into *this*?"

"No, this is the main processor. We need one of the private encrypted nodes. Look, they aren't going to just *let* us in, it will be in a restricted area. We need to create a diversion."

"A diversion?" Raynor smirked. "What am I supposed to do, sing?"

"No," she responded. "Just activate your gravity boots."

"That's it?"

The boots clicked to the floor as he activated them.

Lisa walked up to one of the interfaces and touched it gently. Raynor stayed close so he could watch her in action. She closed her eyes, there was rapid flickering movement behind her eyelids as her consciousness violated the Athenaeum's security protocols. Raynor felt the gravity lift. Gasps and shouts echoed through the chamber as the occupants floated free. People were trying to clutch onto anything fixed to the floor. The gravity on this moon was almost non-existent and the suspension fields normally kept them from floating away. But now, the very same systems were being used against them. Breaching the controls was difficult without permissions. But Lisa didn't stop there. Confusion turned to dismay as the suspension fields created a gravity vortex; swirling currents, ripping people away from their anchors to be tossed around the room like dolls.

"Don't you think this will raise a bit of suspicion?" Raynor asked. "We're the only ones still standing."

"By the time they can do anything about it, I plan to be long gone. So we need to hurry."

She took her hand off the interface and led him up an open staircase to the next floor. The sound of their boots could barely be heard over the commotion and mayhem going on in the main chamber. They went up another level and passed through a security checkpoint, which flashed red. Nobody was there to stop them from entering. Lisa placed her hand on an interface next to a door. She closed her eyes and the door slid open without protest. They walked into the restricted area and saw a smaller data matrix floating above a holographic interface.

Lisa approached and placed her hand inside of it. She closed her eyes. "This is going to require all of my attention, so I will only be minutely aware of my surroundings. If anyone comes through those doors, tap me on the shoulder."

Raynor waited patiently, glancing around at the empty room lined with glowing interfaces. He wondered how long it would take for the Enforcers to be notified and a Technician to correct the gravity. He flicked a bead of sweat from his forehead and watched it drift away under zero-g. Each second ticked over in his mind as he waited nervously for Lisa to get what they needed. The tiny drop of liquid curved down rapidly and splashed on the ground plating. He narrowed his eyes and focused on the blast-door as he reached for his weapon and instantly regretted having to surrender it at the entrance. There was nothing he could do as the squadron of heavily armed Enforcers breached the entry, marched briskly through the doorway and lined the room around them.

"I have it!" Lisa said, finally.

Raynor tapped her on the shoulder.

DATAFILE

Enforcers of Peace

Node 1

An Enforcer of Peace (simply referred to as an Enforcer) is a representative of their Colony responsible for upholding the rules and regulations set out by the Nexus Treaty. They are tasked with maintaining compliance from all citizens in a way which reflects the ethics and values of the Nexus.

Node 5

While the EOP program is an initiative required by the Nexus, each Colony is responsible for training and supporting their own enforcement, who report directly to the Colony's hierarchy. This means that the rules and regulations the Enforcers uphold may be different from one Colony to another. No matter where you are, you must always obey any direction given to you by a Colony Enforcer. Failure to comply may result in heavy penalties, including rehabilitation.

Node 12

Enforcers carry a range of lethal and non-lethal equipment depending on their deployment. This includes Kevlex body armour, quick-deploy energy barrier and a particle-beam blaster.

Node 13

It is important to remember that the Enforcers are there for your protection and the protection of those around you. If you ever feel threatened or unsafe, you are always able to rely on the security and protection of the Enforcers. No matter what level of Value you hold.

CHAPTER SIX

Rescue

Persephone trailed Raynor and Lisa through the central district of Luume. She felt out of place strolling through the green city walkways, wearing all black. Her poor choice of attire for this mission was apparent. Everyone else she passed was wearing light, bright and colourful clothing. The city seemed more an oasis than a mining colony.

She glanced over to check the position of her shipmates. It wasn't hard to pick them out in the sea of colours. They had stopped and appeared to be having a heated conversation that looked like a lover's quarrel. It amused Persephone to watch them together. She thought that perhaps, given a different situation, that there may have been a hint of a spark between the rogue and the cyborg. Persephone's thoughts quickly drifted to her own Unity. Her lovers were all far away on a distant planet. She longed to return home to Mars to see them. She even wished that Raynor would join them, but he never expressed an interest in having anything more than they already had. It was good company and good sex. That was all.

She perused the garments at a promenade stall. She ran her hand over the soft fabrics and paused over a colourful dress with blue, white and green flower patterns. She checked the size and held it up over her blacks, confirming her choice in a mirrored surface. A touch of her Link against the virtual assistant confirmed the cross-colony acquisition.

She removed her jacket and pulled the dress on over her black top, then discreetly wriggled out of her cargo pants. They stowed neatly in her weapons pack slung casually over one shoulder.

Checking on the quarrel; Lisa was walking away from Raynor, her hands clenched into fists. It was just like him to say the wrong thing. But Raynor followed her into a large dome-topped building near the centre of the city.

Persephone looked around the surrounding walkways lined with trees. She spotted a curvy monument in the centre of a grassy patch, obviously intended for sitting, and so she made herself comfortable. To pass time, she pulled out her Link and flicked through her messages on the holographic display. They were posts from friends and family, doing things that they enjoyed and the brief glimpses into their lives made Persephone smile.

She startled back to reality when an armoured vehicle descended, spilling a squad of Enforcers into the street. Her position was directly between them and the entrance to the Athenaeum and they were heading right toward her. She flicked through the device menu on her Link and attempted to contact Raynor, but the call wouldn't connect. She had to act fast. Maybe if she could create a diversion, she could keep the Enforcers busy long enough for Raynor to escape. Her next call was to *Galaxy*.

"Red, I need your help!"

"What is it I can help you with, Persephone?"

"I'm in the no-go with a bag full of questions, surrounded by a whole bunch of unfriendlies. Can you get me out?"

"You're going to have to let them catch you," said the A.I. "You packed a high yield shock grenade in your pack. I suggest you use it. Now."

"At this range it will take me out, too."

"You're going to have to trust me."

Persephone looked up. They were getting closer. She reached into her bag and gripped the fist sized sphere. She let the bag fall to the ground and in one seamless motion, twisted the sphere, pressed the detonation sequence and under-armed it into the squad. The action was so fluid that she could have been picking a flower off the ground. She only had to give the charge a gentle push in the right direction and its own built-in motor did the rest.

The grenade found its mark and erupted with an ear-shattering boom before any of them had a chance to react. The force sent them all flying into the air. Persephone was thrown backwards and hit the ground hard.

When she awoke, she was surrounded by Enforcers talking amongst themselves.

"Do you think she's involved with what's going on inside?"

"Doesn't look like it. She's a Martian, just been reported for dereliction. She must have thought we were coming to arrest her."

"How's that for irony. I'll see her back to her ship while you lot sort out the Athenaeum."

"So, we're not going to take her back for questioning?"

"No. We have bigger issues, and the last thing we want to do is—"

"What's going on?" Persephone asked groggily.

"Internal Colony affairs, nothing for an outsider to be concerned about. But it appears as though someone's been looking for you."

"Yeah, and they are quite anxious to have you back! Been skipping out on your duties, have you?"

One of the Enforcers picked up her bag. "Why don't we hold on to this for a little while? We don't want anyone to get hurt."

Persephone looked from one to another, trying to appear helpless. "What are you going to do with me?"

"Normally, we'd detain you for attacking Colony Enforcers. But your C.O has put out a recall notice. Dereliction of duty *and* stolen weaponry! Pretty serious," one of them said.

"Not our problem, though," another one said, restraining her wrists. "We've got more important things going on. Enforcer 885 will take you back to your ship."

The ride back in the cruiser was brief and uneventful, but for the news she heard on the Enforcer's Link that two individuals from the Athenaeum had been taken into custody with no casualties. Enforcer 885 walked her up the access ramp of *Galaxy* to a stern-faced Rob, standing in the lobby.

"Thank you for your assistance, Enforcer. She wasn't any trouble, was she?"

"Trouble? Her little stunt interfered with a tactical response, costing us valuable time. In fact, it's a good thing you acted swiftly in reporting her. Otherwise, she may have ended up as a person of interest in our investigations."

"Is that so? Sounds like something quite serious must have happened."

"No, no, it's all under control now. Nothing to worry about."

"Very good then," Rob said. "I can take it from here."

The Enforcer removed Persephone's restraints and returned to his Cruiser. Rob watched in silence as the vehicle lifted off and whizzed away. "Well, that was lucky," he said, finally.

"Lucky? They've captured Raynor. How is that lucky? We have to help him!"

"And how do you suppose we do that? Break into another secure Saturn Alliance compound? Because that worked out *so well* for us the first time."

"We can't just leave him there to fend for himself! I'm guessing they had to fake their identities to get into the Athenaeum, but as soon as the Enforcers figure out who they really are…"

"It sounds like you brought them some time to get what they were after. Hopefully, they got it!" Rob smiled at her through his thick brown beard. "Raynor has all the tools he needs to escape on his own. If he needs any help, he will come and get us."

"How will he do that if he is detained?" Persephone gasped. "Don't you get how serious this is?" Rob had turned away, but Persephone wasn't finished. She yelled out to him. "What about Diputs?"

"There is nothing either of us can do at this time. I suggest you get some rest and wait for Raynor."

Persephone waited for Rob to leave, picked up her pack, and headed straight for the exit. She crossed the lobby in a couple of strides but came to an abrupt stop at the doorway. The force of a suspension field pushed firmly against her.

"Red, what are you doing?"

"I'm sorry Persephone, but Rob has instructed me not to let you leave."

CHAPTER SEVEN

Prisoners

Lisa knew from her internal chronometer that she has been in her cell for three hours, forty-seven minutes and eleven seconds. It wasn't comfortable—it wasn't meant to be. The tiny cubicle was used as an intimidation device. There was no light and she had neither enough room to stretch her slender body out fully, or even stand up without crouching. The walls and floor weren't flat, rather they had an assortment of weird angles, points and grooves, like some sort of digital mountainscape, so that there was no way to lie down comfortably.

Lisa could sense something else. A weak psionic wave pushed at her mind, trying to make her docile. She fought against it, her own nanites creating a frequency to block it. Lisa surmised that the average person would break quickly in a place like this.

She had tried her Link, but there was no connection. No surprise. The cell only opened from the ceiling and was manually latched from the outside, so she couldn't hack into it. It seemed like there was no way for her to escape under her own power.

A deep disembodied voice asked into the darkness. "Who are you?"

"Let, me, out!" Lisa pounded her fists on the wall as she said each word.

"Who sent you to attack the Athenaeum?"

This time she said nothing. She just waited in the silence for the next prod. An electrical current surged through the walls and floor of the cell. Her extremities tingled as the energy entered her body, looking for a place to ground. Instead, dermal sensors registered the current, routed it through her capacitors and absorbed the electricity into her storage cells. She traced the current back to its source and reached for more. Drawing out every bit of energy she could. A sense told her that systems around the building were starting to fail as she greedily absorbed power. Then finally, she gave it all back. Like unleashing a torrent, the energy surged back into the wireless veins of the structure, triggering the safety protocols on every device to cut them out of the grid.

It took them a little while to recover. "Who are you?" the voice asked again, harsher this time. "Your silence doesn't help you, terrorist. Tell us what we want to know, and we will apply leniency with your sentencing."

This was what she was waiting for. Now she could make the demands. "Let me out! I want to speak to your commanding officer. My name is Lisa Separa, Observer for Mars. I'm protected by the Nexus treaty!"

"That's not what your Link says; *Annabelle Waters*. Who we know has been dead for eight rotations. Why should we believe you? Who *really* sent you?"

"Nobody sent us. We act of our own volition."

"So, you admit to planning this attack on the Colony yourself?"

"It wasn't an attack," she insisted.

"You infiltrated a restricted Colony building with faked records and attacked our people while attempting to gain access to protected information. You're looking at total reconditioning right there."

"We were trying to track down an outlaw infestation, right here, in this city."

"There is no outlaw infestation," the voice denied angrily.

"The files I was accessing were for an underground military installation that has been hidden from all public records. If it is not outlaws, then what is the Saturn Alliance trying to hide down there?" No answer. Lisa placed her hand against the top of her cell. She closed her eyes and focused on the almost undetectable vibrations emanating from outside her prison. Her internal processors interpreted the vibrations and converted them to words.

"What if she is right about there being outlaws in Luume? We recently had a report of an abduction in the Sanctuary."

"The files she was trying to access are encrypted and require top level clearance. Even if she is telling the truth about an installation down there, we are better off passing this up the chain of responsibility. Alert the Commander to see if he wants to send someone to interrogate her further."

Lisa took her hand away. If this underground installation really was the Saturn Alliance's doing, then she needed to uncover what they were up to and convey the information to Swift.

She banged on the top of the cell angrily. "Let! Me! Out! I'm an Observer! Holding me captive like this will only make things worse! You don't want that, do you?" There was no response.

Several hours passed with Lisa lying uncomfortably on the uneven floor of her cell. She needed sustenance. A tube of Organix to keep her non-mechanical organs functioning. "How long are you going to keep me in here?" she asked into the silence. "I need something to drink."

A force pressed down on her. She began to feel so heavy that she could no longer lift her arms off the floor. Light cracked in from the four sides of the ceiling and the entire panel slid away. She struggled against the force, even though she knew it was futile. A uniformed Enforcer stood over her cell. He looked at her with a stern expression and tossed down the much needed Organix before closing the cell again. Once the panel was securely in place, the suspension field was lifted. She eagerly drained the tube of liquid sustenance.

She hated feeling so useless. She wondered if there was something she could have said that might have given her a better outcome. There was no point beating herself up about it. They would have to let her out eventually. She was an Observer. Sooner or later, Swift would come looking for her. Then there would be trouble.

The cell cracked open again, but this time the suspension field was not activated to hold her in place. Had they forgotten? She shifted her weight, ready to spring out the second the panel was slid open. As her window to freedom got bigger, it was Raynor's face she saw crouched down over her prison.

"What? How did you..." Lisa thought of the device he had used back when they escaped the outlaw-controlled battleship *Pywayrah*. Rob had originally told the Colonies that the rare fuel source used to power the Star was expended, and the device was now useless. Was it possible they had come across more? Had they found another way to power it? Or, was it just another deception? Either way, she didn't expect to get a straight answer out of him.

"I'll explain later," Raynor said. Before she could object, he grabbed her by the wrist and pulled her out of the cell, in close to him. He put his other arm around her in an embrace and then reality started to fade away. With a flash, her thoughts, ideas and everything that made her who she was flowed freely around the room. The sensation was what she expected dying would feel like. It was the same as the first time she had used the Star with Raynor to escape *Pywayrah*. Her body no longer existed, and nothing stopped her mind from spilling out.

Just like before, she felt Raynor's presence surrounding her. It was like he encapsulated her with who she was and defined her in a bubble of thought. She wanted to perceive him and know who he was. To use the lack of boundaries to uncover his secrets. But she could barely perceive herself in that moment, let alone delve through Raynor's thoughts.

She felt him pulling her along, or maybe he was pushing her. But they were moving, in a way that time and distance didn't seem to hinder. They left the cells behind, with the bewildered Enforcers who had witnessed their transformation, and spilled out into a space that she could not see but was intimately aware of.

They brushed people's awareness as they moved, quick as lightning through the city. Lisa felt as though she knew each of them personally as she touched their minds for the briefest of instants. A man who was desperately infatuated with impressing a woman whom he saw every rotation on his walk to work—but thought he would never be good enough for her. A woman who was struggling to cope with her Unity with four other people as well as strenuous demands of her position. Lisa could feel the woman's anguish at the situation before her. She felt lost, like she was just another number. She felt unimportant at work and at home. She wondered if anyone would miss her if she ran away and started a new life in a new colony.

Then, just as quickly; Lisa snapped out of this infinite awareness. Colours and emotions flashed by as they flowed into the underground tunnels that led to the hidden complex. Lisa managed to find the information that she had gathered from the data node from her own awareness and pushed it towards her perception of Raynor.

She opened her eyes and saw the polished stone walls around her. She felt that she knew this place in such detail that it was like returning home. A pang of loneliness slammed into her like a Transway carriage moving at top speed. The sudden isolation in her own mind was as constraining as the Enforcer cell she had just left. She looked at Raynor with a new sense of caution as she struggled to reorder her scrambled thoughts. The level of power the Star contained was immense. And in that instant, she knew why he and Rob had lied to their superiors to protect the device from being exploited.

Raynor appeared to have composed himself much quicker. "I'm going to get some backup," he said. "Lay low until I get back."

"Wait!" Lisa said. "When you get back, we need to talk about that... thing."

Light flared around him. Lisa shot up an arm to shield her eyes. It was like being hit with a sharp reflection of the sun. By the time her eyes had adjusted he was gone, leaving her alone in an enemy stronghold to fend for herself.

CHAPTER EIGHT

Devotion

Diputs wandered through the polished stone hallways alone. No one attempted to stop him. He walked up to an interface, looked around carefully then tapped to access a map of the facility. He made mental note of the path he needed to take and walked further along the corridors towards two large metal doors. Two guards approached; particle beam rifles casually slung over their shoulders.

"Where do you think you're going?" one said. "This area is off-limits."

"I am looking for Serena's family," Diputs replied. "Do you know where I can find them?"

"Serena?" One shrugged. "Who's that?"

"They are definitely not in there," the other said.

Diputs placed one hand on his hip and gestured with the other for them to get out of his way. "Look, Evon said I could walk around freely. So what's the problem?"

"Boss said the hangar is off limits to you. Try the Gardens."

Diputs hesitated. "Isn't Evon the boss?"

The guards glanced at each other. One of them shook his head and said sharply, "Brastar is the Facility Overseer."

Diputs turned around and walked off. He realised at that moment he wasn't really as free as he had been told. Either Evon still didn't completely trust him, or this Facility Overseer had even more influence than Evon.

Diputs meandered through the corridors, looking for Serena's family. He had to convince them to leave this place before things got messy. He couldn't fail them like he had Serena. Another study of the map indicated where the living areas were. The room where he was being kept was part of the communal lodgings. There was also an underground garden where people went for personal reflection. He searched both but found no sign of Serena's parents.

Finally, after what felt like hours of wandering aimlessly, he found them walking to their lodgings.

"Resden! Avilen! I'm sorry, but you're not safe here," Diputs yelled. His voice reverberated through the corridors.

"Excuse me?" Avilen asked in a shaky voice.

"We have never been safer!" Resden exclaimed. "At least, we *were*, until they brought *you* here."

"Do you think I want to be here?" Diputs snapped.

They drew back, eyes glancing down at the amulet Evon had bestowed on him. Feeling self-conscious about its implications, he tucked it into his robe. "The Colonies *will* find this place. It's only a matter of time." He tried to reach out to them. "Come with me! You would be safe on *Galaxy*. Mars would take you in, I'm sure of it."

"Did you make Serena the same offer before you got her killed?" Avilen asked bitterly.

"I did," he said. "Before she got *herself* killed."

"The Divine had a path set out for us to follow, and you interrupted it," Resden said. "If you hadn't got in the way, things would be very different."

"Have you ever considered that me being here now *is* part of the Divine plan?" Diputs said ironically. Serena's parents looked at each other, as if they were exchanging a silent conversation, but they didn't answer him. "I'm devastated about what happened to Serena I really am. I never wanted any of this to happen. But this is not the end! You still have another daughter and you still have each other! Don't throw that all away for what amounts to insanity."

"Insanity?" Resden hissed. "Our faith is *not* insanity. And we cannot abandon our faith, not now. Not in these dire times."

"Now we must see where it leads us and follow it through to the end. Sol deserves that," Avilen finished.

Diputs realised he was getting nowhere. He was determined to do everything in his power to get Serena's family out of this mess before they were hurt, or worse, killed.

"See this?" Diputs clutched the amulet, shaking it in their faces. "Evon said I am the chosen one, and he made me your leader. I speak for the light now. And I say we need to get out of this place."

Resden shook his head. "Brandishing a shiny trinket doesn't make you a leader. If that is what the Divine wants for us then it will be so."

With that, they passed him and continued without looking back. Diputs gripped the amulet and squeezed it until it hurt. Why did Evon think he could lead an entire community of outlaws to safety? He couldn't even get Serena's parents to follow him. How could he possibly be *the chosen one*? He decided he needed to speak with Evon again. There must be something he could offer the Divine Cleric in exchange for releasing Serena's family from this mind control.

He strode purposefully through the winding stone passageways that led up to a higher level near to the top of the complex. Though he passed several people, he couldn't shake the feeling he was being watched. Every time he looked over his shoulder, *someone* was there. He quickened his pace.

The wall mounted interface told him which chamber belonged to Evon. He wasn't surprised when he entered the antechamber. It was saturated with a warm orange glow, giving the room a soothing quality. The same polished stone walls were decorated with lush draping fabrics and colourful artwork. It was certainly a lavish entranceway for someone with no Value. But what need did one have for Value when they were not a subject of the Colonies? Evon had an army of followers to get him anything he wanted. That in itself was more valuable than any display of material possessions.

Diputs froze when he entered the main living chamber. It was no less opulent than the previous room. It was larger and contained an enormous bed covered in blankets and pillows. Diputs was yanked backwards. Someone quite strong grabbed him, swung him around and slammed his face against the wall.

"What are you doing here?" a raspy voice asked.

Diputs felt the cold kiss of a blaster against his neck and the pressure of the man's forearm pushing into his back. "I'm not here to steal anything. I was just looking for Evon."

The pressure eased, so Diputs turned around to face his attacker—a tall, sturdy man, with a square-jawed face; mostly shadowed by his robe. His chin further darkened by a layer of stubble. Diputs shook himself free of the man's grip and fixed up his own dishevelled robes. "Who are you?"

"I am Cleric Calton Brastar." A look of realisation and Brastar lowered his weapon. "And you are the so called *chosen one.*" He tipped back his hood to reveal a shiny bald head and beady eyes. This was the Facility Overseer the guards had spoken of.

Brastar turned his gaze to the amulet hanging around Diputs' neck. "Where did you get that?" He lifted the amulet, taking a closer look at the golden sun. Diputs grabbed hold of the chain and gently pulled it back.

Brastar suddenly yanked the amulet free from Diputs' grasp and the chain whipped away. "*This* should be mine," Brastar said, holding it up to the light. "Evon has held it for far too long."

Diputs crossed his arms. "What do you want with it?" He thought back to Resden's parting words. *Brandishing a shiny trinket doesn't make you a leader.*

Brastar smiled greedily as he stuffed it in his pocket. "It is the key to receiving the blessing of the Divine. It is my purpose."

"So, this is why you were following me? Just say I let you keep it. I want something in return."

Brastar scratched his chin. "Let me keep it?? What are you going to do, take it back?"

"Well," Diputs said. "Maybe we can help each other."

Brastar grinned. "How could you possibly help me?"

"By not interfering. I can only assume that you need the amulet to usurp Evon, which would work better if it were a surprise."

"I could always just kill you right now."

"Sure you could. But then, who would follow the heretic who murdered the chosen one? Look, I don't care who leads these people. What I want is for Resden, Avilen and Romea to be free from all of this. I want them to come with me to safety, but they refuse. They need someone to tell them that is the desire your Divine Light wants."

Brastar was no longer grinning. "Get out of here, and hope you never meet me again."

Brastar pushed past Diputs, leading with a hard shoulder. "If you warn Evon, I'll have you both killed. It won't make any difference."

Diputs left the chamber wondering how he could turn this situation into an advantage. Maybe Serena's family wouldn't want to follow Brastar.

CHAPTER NINE

Rescue

The thrill of Star travel rushed through Raynor's awareness. He knew Persephone and Jake felt the same, but he did his best to block out their thoughts. The danger of travelling this way, as Rob had warned him, was that as they all became light, there were no physical boundaries holding in their thoughts and keeping them together. Raynor felt like he had to bundle up everything that made him who he was and hold it tight in his awareness. Not just for himself, but for Persephone and Jake as well. It took considerable effort. But if he didn't, it would be too easy for them to just slip away, unconstrained.

The transition back to solid matter wasn't painful in the traditional sense. But rather, it was an insult to the euphoric state of existing as pure energy. It was a change Raynor was becoming increasingly reluctant to make. He just chalked it up to being another cost of using the experimental technology. Persephone inspected her hands and beamed with astonishment. Raynor realised it was her first time travelling this way. Jake, on the other hand. While having done this once before, was still in the corner emptying the liquid contents of his stomach. Blue Organix. It looked no different from when Jake drank it before their trip.

"Didn't you say Lisa would be waiting for us?" Jake asked.

Before Raynor could answer, Lisa came rushing through the door with blood on her hands. The abrupt intrusion caused them all to draw their weapons.

"What's the matter?" Raynor asked. "What did you do?"

"I encountered some hostiles," she said flatly. "One of them is dead."

"And the others?"

"Unconscious. I locked them both in a vacant room. But if they get out or are discovered..."

"I don't plan to be here long enough for that to become an issue," Raynor said.

"I know where we can get clothes," Lisa said, motioning forward. "If we blend in it will be easier to move around. But that's not going to stop someone from realising that you don't belong, so try to be as inconspicuous as possible."

Lisa led the way. She stopped periodically to check the corners for passing traffic and then glanced back to ensure they were all still following her. "The data I retrieved from the secure Node included a floor plan. There are no obvious places to keep prisoners, so we need to split up and each search an area which they might use. Jake, you should stay around here to search the storage and maintenance areas. Raynor, you should take the living areas. Persephone, there is an infirmary two levels directly below us. If he is hurt, they may be keeping him there."

"Well, look at you, giving out orders," Raynor grinned. "And what will your part be in this *master* plan?"

"I will search the main hangar and laboratories. That will allow me to find out what is really going on down here."

No guards were encountered on the way to the laundry. The door slid away with a hiss. They entered a warm room with floor-to-ceiling shelves stacked with neatly folded garments.

"Still nobody around. Are we just lucky?" Raynor asked.

"Let's hope it continues," Lisa said. "Got any more auspicious devices up your sleeve?"

Raynor shook his head. "What exactly do you expect to find?"

"I don't know yet," Lisa admitted as they wrapped each other in the robes. "Soldiers dressed as outlaws?" She pulled a thick purple hood over her head and transformed into one of *them*. "Look. I think you were right about the Saturn Alliance being up to something. All the files around this compound were heavily protected. But it makes sense; If you wanted to cause tension between colonies without suffering the consequences, you'd just need to convince everyone it was outlaws. But we need more proof."

Raynor nodded. "And what do you suppose they want with Diputs?"

"Exactly," Lisa said. "But that could just be incidental. But we aren't going to find out hanging around in the storeroom. Let's meet back here in two hours."

Persephone, Jake and Lisa had ghosted away, leaving him alone. He heard the door slide open again, but the shelving blocked his view of the entrance. He flicked his hood up, crouched down and pulled at his robes, trying to reach the knife in his utility belt. He waited silently for whoever it was to come closer. If it were his shipmates, they would have announced their return. He found his blade and waited as the footsteps tapped closer. His target rounded the corner, he sprung up and pinned the startled woman against the wall with one hand over her mouth and the other holding his knife at her throat.

It was Raynor's turn to be startled. He jumped back in surprise as the deep blue eyes of a dead woman stared at him with a fearless intensity.

She didn't scream for help. He quickly regained his composure and pressed her against the wall again.

"You're Serena's sister," Raynor said. He felt foolish as soon as the words left his lips.

She cautiously nodded.

"Promise not to scream?"

Again, she gave him a short nod. He opened his fingers but continued to press her head against the wall with minimal force. "Do you know where Diputs is?"

"Are you here to steal him away from us?" she asked innocently.

"Steal him away from *you?* You stole him first!"

"Diputs is *meant* to be here. It is the will of the Divine," she said softly.

"Well, that may be. But it's *my* will that you take me to Diputs. And since I'm the one with the knife, there is only one other way that this will end."

She took a shuddering breath. Fear washed over her face as his threat sank in.

"If you try to escape me, I will kill you," Raynor said slowly. "If you try to alert anyone we pass, I will kill them and then you. Do you understand?"

He wondered if he actually had it in him to follow through with his threat. He hoped that he wouldn't have to find out. It wouldn't be the first time that he had taken a life. But never had he done it in cold blood.

Serena's sister nodded slowly, so Raynor released his hold. She looked at him differently now. No longer did fear resonate from her. Raynor thought that she was silently judging him as a bad person. She reached up slowly and placed both hands on the hood covering his face. "No one usually wears the hood up," she said as she gently pushed it back off his head.

Raynor ran his fingers through his messy hair. "Now, take me to Diputs."

Serena's sister led him out of the laundry into the open corridors. She walked briskly ahead of him, but not so fast that he couldn't keep up or draw attention to them. His robes managed to conceal the knife in his hand. They passed some other people, that gave him strange looks, as if trying to remember who he was and coming up empty. But Serena's sister just smiled at them, even greeting some merrily as they passed.

"What is your name?" Raynor asked her when no one else was around.

She hesitated. "Why do you want to know? Wouldn't that make it harder to kill me?"

"It wouldn't stop me," he admitted.

"Romea," she said, as if giving up a secret. "And yours?"

He thought about lying but wondered if there was any reason why not to tell her. Was there really any way she could use that information against him?

Romea looked at him, probably not sure what to make of his hesitation. "So, I can't know the name of my executioner?"

Raynor cringed at the label. "It doesn't have to be like that, Romea. I'm just here to find my friend. And if you help me, I won't harm you."

"The name of my merciful captor, then?"

"...Raynor!"

But the voice didn't come from him. Raynor and Romea both spun around to see Diputs' face light up.

"Diputs!" Raynor said, relieved. "What is going on? We came here to rescue you."

Diputs looked warmly at Romea. "I see you two have met."

"I was—" Romea began.

"Romea was helping me look for you."

Romea looked at him through narrowed eyes. "Yes. I was bringing him to see you."

"There are guards at the perimeters that stop me from leaving," Diputs said. "But otherwise, they don't seem to be threatened by me wandering around most of the place."

"Their mistake," Raynor said. "Let's get to the others and be away from here before they know what's going on."

"No, wait," Diputs replied. "I can't leave without..." He glanced at Romea.

"Who, *her*?" Raynor asked, waving his knife in her direction. "Bring her then."

"Really?" Romea protested. "I'm not leaving."

"Not just her," Diputs said. "It's Serena's family. I owe them."

"They knowingly sent their daughter to commit an act of terrorism, what could you possibly owe them?" Raynor said incredulously.

"These people..." Diputs said. "They aren't all bad. They aren't like the hardened outlaws you saw on *Pywayrah*. They just believe in a bunch of stupid—"

"Hey!" Romea interrupted. Raynor and Diputs paused and looked at her.

"They chose this," Raynor said. "It's not our place to get involved here. How do you think you are even going to help them? You heard her. She doesn't want to leave. What are we going to do, kidnap her whole family and lock them up on *Galaxy*?"

"You don't understand," Diputs pleaded. "There is more going on. They are building weapons down here. Weapons they are going to use against the Colonies."

Raynor said nothing. He was starting to think it wasn't going to be as easy as he had hoped.

"The guy who kidnapped me, Evon, he says he knew my parents. He thinks I can help them, that I am chosen."

"Chosen? For what?"

"They believe in a supreme being. The Divine. I don't know, it has something to do with light and burning people. But Evon is their leader, for now, and I think he will listen to me."

"So what, you tell him not to attack the Colonies, then just pack up and go home? Diputs, I really can't see it ending the way you want it to." Raynor looked at Romea, aware she was intently absorbing their conversation.

"No, it won't be that easy," Diputs said. "There are some who don't want to follow Evon anymore. That's why he needs me. He thinks that I can convince them to do the right thing. Raynor, I am no leader. How can I convince these people not to fight the Colonies?"

"I don't know much about outlaw politics. I thought they were all just a bunch of delusional cold-blooded killers. What about if you challenged Evon in a fight to the death for the leadership?"

"*We're* the cold-blooded killers?" Romea interrupted. "Is *everything* about killing with you?"

"Come with me to see Evon," Diputs suggested. "I think he will help us. He just wants to stop his followers from getting wiped out."

"This is a really bad idea," Raynor said. But he wondered if it might be a good opportunity to get close to the head outlaw without the protection he had last time. Raynor gripped the knife, still concealed by his robe and silently rebuked himself. Perhaps Romea was right about him. "Fine, take me to see this *Evon*."

Romea and Diputs looked at each other hopefully.

"Neither of you has any idea where he is, do you?"

"I am not privy to the Divine Cleric's daily schedule," Romea confirmed. "I'm just a clerical liaison."

"I tried to find him in his chambers, but no luck," Diputs said. "The last time I saw him was in the amphitheatre."

"That is the main temple where we pay tribute to the Light of the Divine," Romea said. "He spends a lot of time there."

They halted after turning a corner, confronted with two armed outlaws blocking their path. They were in combat gear, with the Saturn Alliance sigil on the left shoulder plate of their body armour. Each one held up a particle beam rifle. Raynor recoiled. He knew how powerful they were. "I think we've been discovered," he said.

They turned as one to head back the other way, but two more outlaws had closed their escape. Raynor was ready to fight. He stood back to back with Diputs as the hostiles advanced on them. Raynor instinctively reached for his vanishing-blade sword at his hip, but it wasn't there. He remembered stowing it away safely in his habitat. The knife would have to do. He gripped it tightly, keeping it hidden, waiting for the best time to lunge at the enemy. He had to wait till they got closer. The outlaws cautiously edged towards them.

"We've been tracking you," one said. "There is nowhere for you to run. We are here to take you to the Divine Cleric."

Raynor grinned, discreetly slipped his concealed knife away and tried to take a less threatening stance. "Well then, what are we waiting for? Lead the way."

The guards looked relieved. One of them grabbed him by the shoulder and shoved him down the corridor.

CHAPTER TEN

Plans

Lisa saw few people on her way down from the living areas, where everyone seemed to be headed. She hoped that it meant the end of their work shifts and that the areas she wished to explore would be unattended. Only the labs now stood between her and the hangar.

She easily hacked her way past the locked entrance and surveillance systems, to be rewarded with a dark room of unoccupied interfaces on the other side. She took a data crystal and a tiny transmitter from her pocket, connected them, then placed the device on an interface and it lit up with activity. Lisa went on to explore the labs. The top level was connected to a testing facility, where partially destroyed targets and simple robots lay about haphazardly, but she couldn't see any weaponry left unattended. The next level was a workshop, with large fabrication equipment laying temporarily dormant, but obviously well used. The workshop opened out onto the hangar floor, likewise shrouded in darkness, but for a few dim lights on the high ceiling. Lisa counted at least fifty heavily armed Fighters parked neatly side-by-side in rows on the far side of the hangar. They were not of a design she was familiar with. Small and sleek, with a pointed beak at the front and a large forward-facing window for the single-person pilot's compartment.

Lisa crossed the hangar to take a closer look. At the same time, data was flowing back to her from the crystal she had placed on the lab interface. Technical information was overlaid directly into her optic implants. These things were no ordinary Fighters. They were highly advanced battle-craft. Lisa had never seen this technology before, and yet, here it was, in the hands of outlaws?

Schematics of the fighter flashed over her vision, and she realised just how advanced they were. She took note of all the weaponry; particle-beams, nano-rockets, layered shielding. They could easily stand up to a fleet of almost any size. Each one displayed the Saturn Alliance sigil on the side. The bulky hull behind the pilot housed the deadly array of weapons, powerful thrusters and an engine that could outrun just about any other spacecraft. The lack of wings or fins meant they were obviously designed for space combat, and their size made them nimble enough to fit through compact spaces.

Lisa's heart raced. She needed to get out of this place as soon as possible and report her findings back to the Martian Council. Raynor was right all along: the Saturn Alliance *was* behind this.

She turned to leave and was shocked to find one of the Fighters powered-up and hovering silently behind her. So advanced that it was able to mask itself from her enhanced senses. She instinctively flung herself down to try and get away from it, but the pilot responded by using the craft to effortlessly pick her up with a suspension field and pinned her against the wall.

A voice echoed through the hangar. "I'm surprised you made it this far." It was coming from a shadowy figure beyond the Fighter.

Lisa didn't speak. She couldn't even struggle against the crushing force of the suspension field.

The echoing voice continued. "Let's get a closer look, shall we?"

The Fighter silently hovered closer. It shone a bright spotlight on her, blinding her temporarily.

"A cyborg. Looks like the Colonies have really sent their best tech against us and yet, still failed."

A modulated voice amped through speakers on the Fighter. "Cleric, others have been captured and taken to the command centre, where Evon is interrogating them."

"Release the field. But be ready. Cyborgs are stronger and faster than they look."

She sensed movement as more people emerged from around the hangar and converged on her location. The suspension field dissipated and Lisa fell to the floor where the group awaited her. She directed nanites to her limbs and swung a fist at the closest opponent, catching him in the jaw. He grunted and stumbled away. Several others took his place. She hit one in the stomach, he doubled over in pain. She swung a fist into another's face to do as much damage as possible—A kick from behind took out her back leg. She collapsed backwards and attempted to roll to her feet, but her combatants were too closely packed around her. Punches and kicks came raining down, one after another, pounding her into the ground.

Lisa was only semi-conscious as they dragged her limp body out of the hangar and through the corridors. She could feel her nanites coursing through her veins and felt a slight tingling burn as they worked relentlessly to repair her damaged flesh. Luckily, most of her internal organs were cybernetic, and couldn't be easily damaged. That could soon change though, depending on how they planned to interrogate her. Perhaps afterwards, they might dissect her in their lab to further their own research, she thought, but dismissed it as paranoid anxiety.

She was still feeling groggy as they dragged her through a doorway and dropped her on the floor. She blinked and opened her eyes to see familiar faces looking down on her. Raynor and Diputs were standing in discussion with an older man with more lavish robes than the others. The two men who had carried her in were standing either side of her. One of them was a large solid man with no hair and a rough face; he stood cross-armed. The other was younger with a dark beard and looked slender in his robes. The bald man pushed down on her shoulder with his foot.

"I found this one in the hangar," her captor said. "Why haven't these intruders been restrained?" He gestured at Diputs. "And why is this outsider here? Do we include him in all our deliberations now?"

"What have you done, Brastar?" the older man asked. "These are not intruders. They are our guests. I have asked for their help with the impending raid. Get your boot off her!"

"Guests? These are no guests. This one is a cyborg!" He pressed his boot harder into Lisa. "You have let an Observer infiltrate us, brother. They *are* the raid. If we let her go, the Colonies will know everything that goes on here. She was loading all of our research onto this." Brastar presented the data crystal to the older man.

"Explain this," the older man demanded as he inspected the crystal.

She waited for the betrayal.

"We had to know what we were really getting into," Raynor said. "You don't think we are just going to trust a bunch of outlaws, do you? If you want our help, you'll let her go and tell us every last detail about this operation."

"I've heard enough," Brastar scoffed. "We don't need their help. The fleet is almost ready. We only need one more sub-cycle and then we will be completely prepared for a full-frontal attack on these evil heretics."

"Except for the fact that the Enforcers now know about this little thing you have going on down here and will be marshalling a force against you as we speak," Raynor said.

"Lies!" Brastar shouted. He released his boot from Lisa's shoulder and confronted Raynor face to face. "This compound was established by the Saturn Alliance to build a failsafe in case the other Colonies turn on them. As far as the council knows it's uncompromised. The Enforcers have no reason to be looking into what goes on down here."

"But if the council were made aware that their little project is now home to outlaws, they may want to come and pay you a visit," Raynor said. "We came here to rescue Diputs. We had to have some sort of contingency in the event we were discovered. Since I have not made contact with my ship, they will have sent all of our data on this compound to the Enforcers. Still think I'm lying? There is an attack coming; you need us."

"So, you knew they were outlaws all along?" Lisa asked angrily.

Raynor shrugged it off.

"If that is the case, why warn us?" Brastar asked. "Wouldn't it be better for you to wait until the Enforcers came to eliminate us?"

"I watched Serena die," Diputs said. "I don't want to have to go through that again. My crew are only here because I wouldn't leave without Serena's family. If you want our help, then I want you to ensure they come with us."

Brastar turned to Evon. "Are you listening to this rubbish?"

Evon looked ponderous, but nodded, as if accepting their explanation. "How long do we have?"

Lisa watched from the floor and rubbed her shoulder. She made no move to rise whilst her nanites continued to repair her damaged body.

"I would say you have two rotations at the most," Raynor said. "Given that they don't know exactly what kind of force you have down here, it may take them a little while to bolster their numbers. But when they do come, you can bet they will come in hard and there will be more of them than you could possibly imagine."

"Then we must escape now," Evon said. "Call an assembly to announce our plans." He looked directly at Brastar. Then, to Diputs; "Make preparations for us to come aboard your ship. We will use some of the Fighters to cover our escape."

Brastar grunted. "And who will be the ones who sacrifice themselves so that you can run and hide? We should all stay and fight till the end. Together. *That* is the Divine will!"

Evon cleared his throat. "I speak for the Divine—"

"What about the cyborg? We cannot just let her go."

"Why not? The Enforcers will come regardless," Evon countered. "None of these people are to be harmed. Do you understand?"

Brastar reached for a weapon holstered at his belt. Raynor was quick to react, lunging towards the broad-shouldered outlaw. Brastar grabbed Raynor and twisted, pulling him to the ground. The weapon Brastar had drawn was placed up against Raynor's neck.

"I could *end* you," Brastar growled. "Right here, in an instant."

If Raynor was intimidated, he didn't let it show. He just silently returned Brastar's steely-eyed gaze.

"That's enough," Evon said.

Brastar stood and brushed off his dishevelled Saturn Alliance uniform. He gave a short bow to Evon and then left wordlessly. Lisa watched bitterly as the outlaw left the room. She stood and tried to look fierce as she turned on the others. "You have a *lot* of explaining to do."

DATAFILE

SPEKTR-8 Advanced Fighter

The SPEKTR-8 was commissioned by the Saturn Alliance Strategic Defence Initiative without Nexus approval. Fifty of the spacecraft were constructed in secret in an underground research and development facility underneath Luume on the Enceladus moon. The SPEKTR-8 is still considered to be one of the deadliest assault Fighters in history and has collectively done more damage than any other vessel of its size.

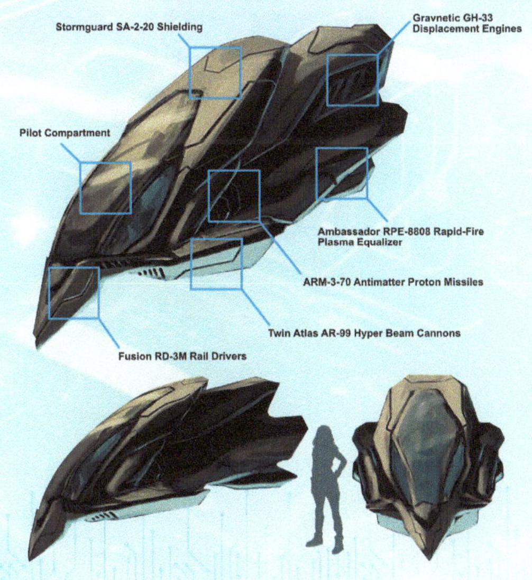

CHAPTER ELEVEN

Challenge

Diputs stood on the dais with Evon and Brastar. Evon was in the middle, Light of the Divine at his back. They watched solemnly as the last of the congregation poured into the amphitheatre. Brastar, now dressed in his ceremonial robes, stepped forward to address the room. He raised his hands into the air. "My brothers and sisters, praise be to the Light of the Divine!" He lowered his hands and continued. "The time for action is near! Our leader, the Divine Cleric, has called this assembly to warn us that the great battle is coming." Brastar turned his head, then smiled deviously at Diputs and Evon. "But instead of fighting it, as the Divine has previously instructed, *he* would have us flee from it. To cower back to the dark reaches of Sol, to be oppressed ever more by the heretics who defy the Divine."

Evon put his hand on Brastar's shoulder to silence him. "This is not—"

"This *is* a challenge!" Brastar went on. "The Light wants us to rise up, not flee. Last night I was delivered a vision by the Divine." Brastar shook himself free from Evon's grip. "In my vision, two seeds were planted. One refused to grow towards the light. It shrivelled up and died. The other stretched out its limbs and was embraced by the light. Even though it was exposed to the harsh weather, the light protected and nurtured it. It grew strong and—"

"This is blasphemy!" Evon thundered. "You do *not* speak for the Divine."

"No, I do not. But the Divine does speak through me," Brastar said. "Which seed are you going to be, Evon? Will you let your cowardice get in the way of our Divine purpose? Or will you lead your people to victory?"

The crowd erupted in a storm of chatter.

"It is true," Evon said. He raised a hand to silence the congregation. "I am no longer the one chosen to lead you to victory. The plan has changed. The Divine has shown us, by sparing the people on the Lunar space station and allowing our plans to fail, that the time is not right. In order to break the clutches of the oppressive Colonies, we must strike at the them when we are at our strongest. Not when we are most desperate."

Brastar said with a sneer, "so, you accept my challenge?"

"If you are going to challenge anyone, you will need to challenge our new leader." He motioned towards Diputs. "Adr—"

"No!" Brastar roared. "*You* will face my challenge!"

Brastar grabbed Evon with both hands and dragged him across the dais, where they were engulfed in the beam of light. Guards had surrounded the dais, preventing anyone from interfering. Diputs didn't know what to do. He wasn't a violent man. But so much depended on the outcome of this moment. Would he be better off being handed the leadership from Evon, or taking it from Brastar by force? He thought about it, he didn't *want* the leadership! But it would give him leverage over Evon, which he might be able to use to find out more about his parents. He told himself that surely, if Evon wanted Diputs to be the leader, then Brastar would be burned in the light. Whatever trickery was at play here, he had to trust that Evon had planned this out. And if not, then he would just have to deal with Brastar. He just had to wait and see what happened.

Brastar held one hand on Evon's face, the other clutched at his throat. Evon struggled and surged against the hold, but Brastar was much stronger. Steam began to rise from Evon's robes and his skin was turning red. A muffled scream rang out from the Divine Cleric as his flesh began to sear and burn under the light. Diputs' heart was racing. This couldn't be part of Evon's plan. Brastar was still unharmed, standing victoriously over his burning adversary. He tossed Evon out of the light beam.

This was it. This was Diputs' moment. He had to challenge Brastar, now. This was what Evon had set him up for. All he needed to do was step up and take the leadership. Diputs took a step towards Brastar. He reached into the light, same as he did before. But this time was different. He instantly felt the heat on his skin. Something was wrong, he recoiled.

The congregation was on their knees giving homage to their new Divine Cleric. Brastar begun to levitate gently above the dais.

"The Divine Light speaks to me," Brastar's voice boomed. "The enemy is upon us. We prepare for battle!" He looked down on Diputs with a sneer from his new position of power. "Now, kill the intruders!"

CHAPTER TWELVE

Execution

Diputs didn't know what they had used to bind his arms behind his back, but it was tight and hurt his wrists. The guards pushed them along in a line. Lisa and Raynor were ahead of him, with Evon at the very front of the procession—with his singed robes and burned flesh. Diputs looked back and saw Persephone and Jake trailing behind. They would all be dead already if Evon had not convinced Brastar that outsiders were not worthy of an execution in such a holy place. Brastar agreed and had them marching to their death.

"How did Brastar get the amulet?" Evon asked Diputs angrily.

"He grabbed it off me in your chambers," Diputs said. "I didn't think it was that important."

"Not *important*? Do you care so little for any gift given unto you?"

"What value would I put on some weird symbol of religious ideology?"

"I gave you that so that you could stop Brastar and take power as the true and rightful chosen one," Evon explained. "Now *he* has it!"

"I told you, I'm not who you think I am," Diputs said.

Evon looked at Diputs with sadness in his eyes. "You really don't know who you are at all, do you?"

The guard next to him asked his colleague, "Where should we do it?"

"Here is as good a place as any," he suggested.

They were in a wide corridor near one of the entrances to the compound. The guards lined them up against the wall.

Diputs turned to Evon. "After you gave me that amulet, I was able to put my hand in the light. I thought for a moment that maybe you were right and that I could make a difference here. But it was all just a trick, wasn't it? Tell me, how did you do it?"

The guards looked at each other, eager to hear what their old leader would confess.

Evon sighed. "I suppose it doesn't matter now. The amulet contains a nano-virus programmed to protect the wearer from the effects of the light beam, which is actually just a supercharged suspension field."

The guards looked confused. But one of them said angrily, "Don't listen to this heretic. He has fallen out of favour with the Divine and now he shows his true irreverence."

"But what if he is telling the truth?" another guard said, hesitantly. "What if this has all been a lie?"

"Do you denounce the Divine based on these lies?" the first guard queried. "Perhaps you should die with them."

"Not denounce, no. But what if the Clerics are misrepresenting the Light? Is this how we are taught to act? So easily they twist the teachings of love and strength to be used for ulterior motives."

"He is with THEM!" shouted the guard. He brought his weapon up, aimed at his comrade. "Kill the non-believers!"

Diputs watched the embers of doubt ignite rapidly amongst them. The other guards stared wide-eyed and quickly chose sides. Their advocate had a blaster of his own, which he pointed defiantly at the head of the group. The rest followed suit, their focus no longer on their prisoners.

From the corner of his eye, Diputs noticed that Raynor had produced a shimmering blade. He swiftly flung the knife at the leader and it landed firmly in the side of the outlaw's head, triggering a volley of weapons fire. Diputs ducked and charged towards a guard head-first to ram into him and throw him off balance. It seemed to have worked because the next thing he knew, Raynor was picking him up off the floor and cutting his bindings.

Diputs assessed the situation. Persephone was suppressing three guards, on their knees, at the end of a blaster. The rest of the outlaws were riddled with holes. Lisa and Jake appeared unharmed, whilst Evon had been grazed by a blaster shot. It had torn his robes and seared the already scorched flesh on his arm.

"What do we do now?" Jake asked.

"We should get out of here," Lisa said. "Let the Enforcers clean up this mess."

"Serena's family is still in there," Diputs objected.

"We cannot abandon these people," Evon said. "I have led them down the wrong path with trickery and deception, it is true. But the Light of the Divine is real. These people do not deserve to be slaughtered by the Enforcers. We need a plan!"

"You mean we need more deception," Diputs said bitterly.

"Exactly! Look, I know you think it's unscrupulous, but these people need signs to reinforce their acts of faith. Being a leader isn't about being a good or honest person. It is about recognising what people need and giving it to them."

"That is just the worst advice, ever," Lisa said.

This was met with a disdainful look from Evon. Raynor, however, looked quite amused.

"Well, you can't use the same 'magic trick' again," Raynor said. "Brastar has your amulet. So where are you going with this?"

"What about those Fighters?" Diputs asked.

"That's exactly what I was thinking," Evon said. "If we can remote access the Fighters, we can make it look like I am controlling them through the will of the Divine."

"Remote access?" Raynor said angrily. "We can't even get a message out and you want us to hack into a fleet of spacecraft?"

"We would only need one," Lisa said. "I could do it. But we need a way to boost the connection and get rid of whatever is blocking the signal." She reached into her pocket and produced a small data crystal. "And I need someone to sneak aboard and attach this to the interface."

"Then you should lead a team to the signal disruptor," Evon said. "I will go to the hangar and cause a distraction while someone sneaks onboard a Fighter. Then on my signal, fire a couple of warning shots to scare them."

No one spoke. Diputs guessed they were all equally reluctant to trust or even follow this madman.

"I really don't care what you do," Lisa said. "I'm not going to help you escape. But I want control of those Fighters, so I'm in."

"Same," Raynor agreed.

"You know what I want," Diputs said. "You agree to that and I'm in."

"Well of course," Evon said. "We need you to take us at least as far as the outer planets."

Diputs grinned. "It won't be a comfortable journey. But we should be able to make enough space for everyone in the cargo hold." He knew they couldn't, but if being deceitful was the characteristic of a strong leader, then it was time for him to step up and become a strong leader.

CHAPTER THIRTEEN

Execution

Lisa placed her hand on the door and closed her eyes. Her mind rendered the digital scape of the isolated control unit. The blue construct consisted of hundreds of floating cubes, each one containing immense code structures. She quickly flicked through each one and reorganised the code. She felt the approval as the right cubes lined up and pulled herself back into her own mind. The door hissed open and they entered, weapons drawn. Persephone took aim at the single guard sitting at a circular interface in the middle of the room. She shot him in the back of the head before he could turn around.

"Ouch..." Raynor said. Persephone turned around and looked at him with annoyance.

Lisa approached the Amplification Stack; a series of rings levitating in a suspension field around a pole that extended from floor to ceiling. Sparks of electricity leapt between the rings as they oscillated up and down, surging with energy.

"As soon as we disable the signal disruptor, we will all be exposed," Lisa said. "To Brastar and to the outside."

Raynor ran his fingers through his hair. "And they will be exposed to us. I can get visuals on everything from this terminal. But we should expect him to come for us pretty quickly."

Persephone took up a defensive position in front of the door and gave the nod.

"I just need you to hold that door for as long as possible," Lisa said. "The piloting system processes billions of lines of code every nanosecond, and I have to try and control that. It will likely take all of my focus just to keep it in the air."

There was one more thing she needed to do once the disruptor went down. With so many hostiles bearing down on them, they needed a way out. She compiled every bit of data she had collected and sent it to Swift. She had to trust he would know what to do.

The hangar was a bustling hub of outlaws going about their jobs. They were working tirelessly on several shells at the end of a long line of finished Fighters. They laboured relentlessly to try and get the fleet ready for battle. Diputs, Evon and Jake hid behind a large crate of machine parts as they pushed it along the hangar, trying desperately to remain unseen. If one of the outlaws recognised Evon, it wouldn't take long for them to be the focus of hostile attention. So, they kept their heads down and put their weight into the heavy container they were pushing towards the nearest Fighter.

Diputs looked over his shoulder to check that Jake was ready for his role—to gain access to the Fighters and connect the data crystal that would bypass their encryption and interface with Lisa.

"Now would be a good time for that distraction," Diputs whispered to Evon.

Evon strode intently into the middle of the hangar, drawing the focus and attention of the workers.

"My people," Evon said in a raised voice that carried easily across the noisy hangar. Every eye was on him and no one seemed to notice Jake scurry up the access ramp at the back of one of the Fighters.

Evon continued. "I live by the will of the Divine light, which shines through me and gives me salvation."

One of the workers began to advance on Evon, but another grabbed his arm and held him back. The rest immediately seemed transfixed by Evon's words.

"It is true, I fell out of favour with the Divine. I was false! Not strong enough to do what was needed myself." Evon raised his hands in the air theatrically. "This allowed Brastar to impose his own agenda. He does not serve the Light. He serves his own selfish desires. He will lead you all to ruin! He doesn't care for your lives! He only wants to cause as much suffering as possible. To go out in a blaze of glory is not devotion, it is an empty sacrifice."

"Better to die fighting than to be shot down while fleeing like cowards," someone shouted.

"But what does the fighting achieve? You are worthless unless your life is given for the Divine, not for your pride."

"How do we know you speak the truth? What proof do you bring that the Divine wills us to follow you?"

"*NOW*, you want to know what proof?"

The Fighter rose abruptly and hovered behind Evon. He gestured towards the empty pilot's compartment.

"It is the will of the Divine that I am still alive," Evon bellowed. "The Light commands this Fighter, this angel of death. There will be no mercy for anyone who does not submit. Kneel down and repent!"

There was a muffled gasp of shock from the outlaws who had gathered closer to see for themselves. Many dropped to their knees. The Fighter rose up and two cannons on the underside of its hull emerged. They flashed with each devastating shot.

CHAPTER FOURTEEN

Purification

The Fighter made short work of the unfaithful outlaws. Diputs choked on the smell of seared flesh and blood. Somewhere, fires were spreading, filling the hangar with a smoky red glow. There were screams, but Diputs could barely hear them over the thunderous fire of the SPEKTR-8's canons.

With Evon's point well and truly made, the shooting ceased, revealing complete devastation. There were dead bodies lying everywhere, mangled and bloody. They were almost unrecognisable as human. Voices could be heard in the grim silence that followed; "Quick!"—"This way!"—"Retreat!"

Diputs watched as several outlaws slipped through an open door on the far side of the hangar and closed it behind them. They had won the hangar. The Fighter powered down and landed gently on the ground. The remaining outlaws who had been smart enough to submit, slowly began to rise out of the carnage. Evon slowly walked around, taking account of their losses. Most of them were severely burned and missing limbs. He still knelt by each one and placed his hand on their body before moving on.

Some wept for the fallen, others just sat in silent disbelief. None of them spoke a word to Evon—the bringer of this destruction. All they could do besides mourn, and comfort was look in horror at the devastation all around them.

"I had hoped that fewer would have thrown their lives away needlessly," Evon said as Diputs approached.

"You make it sound as though you *expected* Lisa would shoot to kill."

Evon rose to meet Diputs' accusation. "She did what she needed to do."

"I wonder if you would still feel that way if they had died for you, rather than Brastar?"

"...died for the Divine," Evon corrected. "I would never ask people to die for me."

"So, what now?" Diputs asked. "We have control of the hangar, but Serena's family are presumably still with Brastar."

Evon placed his hand on the now dormant Fighter. "Brastar will not let them go easily. We don't know who we can trust. The next thing to come through those doors will likely be an attack."

"We can't just leave them behind!" Diputs said.

"We don't have a choice," Evon countered. "I held up my end of the bargain, now you need to make good on yours. Contact your ship, we must round up the survivors and leave immediately."

Diputs gritted his teeth. "The deal was for Serena's family to come with us. Your people are still scattered throughout the complex in service to Brastar! I thought you said you wouldn't leave anyone behind!"

"They have forsaken me! Look around you; those who are left here are not soldiers, they are technicians and workers. What kind of offensive would they inflict on Brastar and those loyal to him? It would only lead to more death. It's a fight we cannot win."

Diputs' Link chimed. Surprised, he pulled it out of his pocket. Raynor was on the display.

"Raynor!" Diputs exclaimed. "Nice work with the signal disruptor. We have control of the hangar."

"We're still in the signal room trying to hold back Brastar's forces. They have us trapped, but we have bigger problems. The Enforcers are approaching from all directions; we'll be completely surrounded. They're going to think we're outlaws."

"What about the Fighters?" asked Evon. "There are few enough of us now that we can use them to escape."

Raynor checked the interface in front of him. "Lisa can only pilot one at a time and she needs to be in here to maintain a strong enough connection."

"The Fighters aren't that difficult to pilot," Evon insisted. "We don't need to fly them into battle, we just need to get free of the Enforcers."

"We have to be able to all get there first," Raynor said.

"No," Diputs said. "We have to surrender to Brastar."

"*What*?" Raynor and Evon said in unison.

"We can't fight the Enforcers. You said it yourself," Diputs turned to Evon. "Brastar has the manpower we need. If we surrender to him, he can fight the Enforcers, just as he wants, and we can escape in the chaos."

"Then what's stopping him from killing us?" Evon asked.

Without any warning, the lone Fighter under Lisa's control powered up again. There was a moment of panic before the hangar erupted with the noise of rail drivers charging. They lit up with energy before erupting into purple beams of light. Diputs leapt for cover.

CHAPTER FIFTEEN

Cleansing

Lisa felt a cold sweat envelop her body as her consciousness returned to the signal room. Her sharp memory saved the faces of each outlaw she had just slaughtered. Technically, Evon had just asked her to scare them. But this was the revenge *she* had sought against the outlaws and those who survived would definitely be scared. Three times now she had been helpless, at the mercy of outlaw terrorism. Now she was the one to bring judgement down on them.

She opened her eyes and took in her surroundings. Persephone had welded the doorway shut. She lay in wait like a hunter, for Brastar and his men to force it open. Raynor was still manning the primary interface, talking through his Link.

She heard Evon's voice come through clearly. "What about the Fighters?" he asked. Evon kept talking, but it was the first comment which stuck in Lisa's mind. The Fighters were the whole issue. In the hands of the outlaws they would be used to slaughter the colonists and destroy Luume before moving on to cause untold damage. In the hands of the colony, they would be used to tip the balance of power for whoever possessed them, probably leading to all-out war.

She suddenly didn't care about Evon or Brastar or even the Saturn Alliance Enforcers. She knew what she had to do. She closed her eyes once more and embraced the seductive temptation of the signal amplifier, her bridge to the advanced Fighter. Data surged through her and she was engulfed once more in the metal embodiment of death.

She charged her weapons, targeted each of the deadly machines and methodically fired on them. Without power, their armoured hull plating was no match for her high-velocity rail-drivers. Their volatile power cells erupted in balls of green fire, ripping the Fighters apart and engulfing the Hangar.

CHAPTER SIXTEEN

Sanctions

The air-car landed on the open platform atop Nexus headquarters on Mars. The building seemed to defy gravity, peeking out from atop the clouds. A few other structures enjoyed the same scene of a fluffy white sea of dense vapour, obscuring their view of the planet beneath. Swift stepped out of his vehicle onto the landing pad and felt the brisk chill of the atmosphere, which was held tenuously in place by a series of suspension fields. He entered the building and was immediately greeted by a stern-faced woman in a Martian uniform.

"I'm Representative Sharin Leam. It's nice to meet you. I assume you know why they have called this meeting?"

"You're new," Swift said.

"Yes. Is that a problem?" She seemed to have a fierce defiance in her voice that reminded him of Lisa.

"That depends on how well you handle yourself in there. Just act like you are in on the joke and let me do the talking."

"So? How do you plan on responding to the accusations? Is it true that we have operatives working in the Saturn Alliance?"

"Just as true, I'm sure, that they have operatives here."

Leam raised an eyebrow. "That's going to be your defence? That won't be good enough, I'm afraid."

"Just trust me. I have some good information to help our case."

The grand oak doors to the council chambers slid away silently in an instant. Swift and Leam entered the round, open room. The sun streamed into the chambers from skylights above, and seats surrounded an extravagant oval table in the centre. Swift noticed Clarissa Dalton occupying one. The most recent instatement from the new United Advancement Entity. Of all the boring, mostly old faces, she was the only Peacekeeper he actually liked.

All eyes were on Swift as he approached an empty chair and sat down. Leam sat in a spot next to him.

"Well, I assume you haven't called me all the way here for a nice little chat," Swift said. "Let's get to the point, shall we?"

"You're quite right, Swift," said Peacekeeper John Dalton. "We have received evidence of quite a troubling nature. A Martian agent; your own Observer, has been apprehended after allegedly infiltrating and attacking a Saturn Alliance Secured-Node on Enceladus."

"Allegedly?" Swift asked.

Zarax Pilar sat with his elbows resting on the table, fingers locked. "There are eyewitness accounts from a score of people that two individuals, one of them a cyborg, entered the Central Athenaeum in the city of Luume." He inhaled sharply and continued. "They caused a gravimetric disturbance in order to gain access to classified information regarding the colonies' infrastructure."

Swift tried to appear genuinely shocked. "That's terrible! Was anyone hurt?"

"No," Pilar admitted with disdain.

"You have video footage, then? Authenticated access logs? Any sort of digital proof of what happened?"

"It would seem that the Cyborg covered her tracks, digitally anyway. But we have footage from armour-cams from the Enforcers placing her at the secured node."

"That's incidental, it doesn't prove an attack."

"The suspects were caught in the act and taken into custody."

"So you have them still? And a confession to go with it?" Swift pressed.

"No," said Pilar. "They happened to escape, despite all the odds."

"Sheer incompetence, that's what it is," Clarissa said. "Why are we wasting our time and Swift's with this complete cock-up of a hearing? Give us something concrete so that we can deliberate and go home." Swift shot her an approving smile.

John Dalton slammed his fist down on the table. "Swift, do you or do you not deny that Mars has committed an unprovoked attack on the Saturn Alliance?"

"I deny it."

"So, what say you against the allegations?"

"Well, since there is no solid evidence of an attack, no real damage, no casualties of any sort and not even a shot fired. I would say they are unfounded."

"This is absolute crap," Pilar insisted. "You can't just dismiss over fifty witnesses and reports that a cyborg hacked into a secure S.A. Node and stole restricted information."

"I'm not denying the event happened," Swift said. "I'm denying it was an unprovoked attack."

"Stealing sensitive data is still considered an attack," John Dalton said.

"What was stolen?" Swift asked.

"What do you mean?" Pillar recoiled. "I just told you. Information."

"No, what exactly was the information that you say they were after?"

"As I previously mentioned, it's classified."

Swift rubbed his chin. "Well then, allow me to help shed some light on this clear misunderstanding."

"Please," Dalton prompted.

"You see, it was *actually* an unsanctioned intelligence-gathering operation." Pilar looked horrified. But before he could say anything, Swift continued. "We had reason to believe that the Saturn Alliance was building a fleet of advanced Super-Fighters that would, if completed, tip the balance of power quite significantly in their favour."

"So, you admit that you sent agents to Enceladus?" Clarissa asked in disbelief.

"I never denied that. Only that it was an unprovoked attack."

"So, this was an unapproved operation, which is still in violation of the treaty," Dalton added.

"Only if without probable cause."

"So then," asked another Peacekeeper, sitting back in his seat. "Can you share with us how you came to suspect the Saturn Alliance of building these weapons?"

Swift produced his Link from his jacket pocket and tapped the surface. "I have just sent you all of the evidence. As you can see, outlaws have infiltrated the Saturn Alliance and they kidnapped one of our skilled Operators. We had to send in a team to try and recover our asset."

"So then why come in here acting so defensive?" Clarissa asked.

"Because that is all he knows," Pilar said, sneering at him from across the table. "He enjoys the drama."

Swift grinned again. "It was important to highlight the sheer treachery of the Saturn Alliance. They are the ones in the wrong here. The whole ordeal with the outlaws was all just misdirection so that they can cover their tracks. I would like the Nexus to impose strict sanctions upon all their operations, pending a full investigation of its leadership and an audit of their resources."

Eyes glanced around the table from Peacekeeper to Peacekeeper.

"I don't think you are in the position to be making demands like that," Pilar said.

"Well," Swift stood, wiping the palms of his hands on his uniform. "Since I've technically just done your jobs for you, I think you probably owe me." He looked around the room. They were all shifting in their seats uncomfortably at the allegations Swift had just brought forward.

"Anything else?" Dalton asked.

"One more thing. I want an immediate intervention and cessation of military action while I extract my agents. If a single Martian is harmed by a Saturnian, then they will feel the full brunt of my forces."

"Very well, Supreme Commander Swift, and Representative Leam," Dalton announced. "You may both be excused while we deliberate and review the evidence you have provided."

"Hurry now, time is of the essence." Swift turned and walked away as the table erupted into chatter.

CHAPTER SEVENTEEN

Hostages

Lisa blinked, getting used to her own eyes again; back in the signal room. She looked around to find Raynor and Persephone at gunpoint, arms raised in the air. Brastar scanned the room with narrowed eyes and scowled. He drew a short-curved blade from his belt and lunged towards her. The blade stopped less than a centron from her throat.

Lisa did not flinch.

"Your friends killed a lot of my people in the hangar…"

"That's unfortunate," she said through gritted teeth. "But we're no good to you dead."

Brastar's knife receded as two outlaws slipped around her to restrain her arms behind her back.

"What were you doing in here? Calling your friends from the colony?" Brastar said with a sneer.

"You bet we did," Raynor said. "You and your people are surrounded. There is only one way out of this."

"So, you're saying we should give up and hand ourselves over?" Brastar said angrily. "The Colonies will never let us walk away. But you are our ticket out of here, is that what you're saying?"

"Not quite," Raynor answered. "What I'm saying is, you have no choices. Come and take a look for yourself."

Brastar walked over to the interface display. He didn't look pleased by what he saw.

"We don't have much time," Brastar shouted. "Get this pathetic unworthy scum down to the hangar."

Once they arrived, Brastar slammed his fist on the large hangar doors. "Open up, Evon."

There was no immediate answer.

Brastar had lined up his bargaining chips. Persephone and Raynor stood with Lisa next to three outlaws. Lisa looked down the line and noticed their resemblance to the girl they had brought here for the Dispersion. Without warning, Brastar grabbed Persephone and put his blaster to her head. "What's your name darling?"

Persephone laughed. "I'm *not* your darling, you small pricked pile of outlaw trash."

"You have ten seconds," Brastar shouted at the door. "And then I'm going to shoot this *charming* lady through the head. Got it?" He pressed the blaster harder against Persephone's head and began to count down from ten. He got to three before the door shuddered. It didn't open right away, but slowly a crack appeared and fingers felt their way through it to force the doors open manually. The ragged figures on the other side were scorched and looked utterly defeated.

Brastar lowered his weapon. "That mad bastard…"

Lisa analysed the blackened wreckage of the hangar. Support structures had collapsed, the floor was littered with rubble and bits of machinery. Panels dangled from the walls, hanging from strands of cables. The ceiling was partially caving in above piles of debris scattered throughout the hangar. Those who stood in the aftermath were bloodied and some were missing limbs.

Diputs was still alive. He was one of the few strong enough to loosen the broken doors. But his expression was blank, his clothing was scorched, and he was covered in dust.

"What happened here?" Brastar shouted. "Where's Evon?"

Through the haze and smoke, they could see one last Fighter still intact, surrounded by the metal corpses of the shattered fleet.

Brastar approached it cautiously. As he neared the cockpit, he drew his blaster and opened the hatch. Evon was semi-conscious in the pilot's seat.

"You!" Brastar accused. He pulled Evon away from the Fighter's controls. "It wasn't enough to betray the will of the Divine, but your own people?"

"No," Evon said meekly. "I was trying to stop it…"

Brastar summoned his followers with the flick of a hand and tossed Evon's broken body to the hangar floor. "Hold this double-crossing piece of shit so I can exact my own revenge." Brastar sat down at the controls and the Fighter groaned to life. It hovered just above the ground and the cannons adjusted to take aim at Evon.

"Get down," Lisa yelled. She dropped to the ground and silently reached for the thin thread still connecting her to the bringer of death. She triggered the core overload in the Fighter and braced herself.

It was seconds between Lisa's shouted warning and the green orb that expanded rapidly from the exploding Fighter. Raynor was ashamed by his slow reaction time. He was halfway to the ground when the shockwave picked him up, carried him across the wide corridor and slammed him mercilessly against the wall.

He lost consciousness.

A jolt from Lisa's soft touch on his temples relieved him of his concussion. His eyes burst open and he took a deep, rasping breath. Wordlessly, she helped him to his feet and handed him a particle beam rifle. Raynor checked the charge. Only five shots remained. He tried to scan the room for hostiles, whilst still fighting the blast-fatigue. He picked his way through human remains and spotted Persephone on the ground rubbing her eyes. He made his way over and locked wrists with her to pull her upright. The three of them, stolen weapons at the ready, herded the outlaws together.

Finally, they had gained control and Persephone took watch over the gang of dishevelled outlaws while Raynor assessed the damage. Bodies littered the piles of debris from the destruction. Patches of combustible materials still blazed, adding thick black smoke to the artificial atmosphere faster than the ventilation systems could extract it. The thing that stood out to him the most was a familiar sigil on some of the damaged crates. Crates that were likely used to house and transport the specialised tech required to build such an advanced fleet of Fighters. The mark was one only a rare few people in the Colonies would recognise; an 'A', circled, with the number '4' overlapping it.

Raynor was so absorbed that he jumped when he heard the crash of the entry charges and shouts of the Enforcers as they stormed the hangar. There was a series of noise deadening bursts from the dampening-grenades that drowned out the shouts and weapons fire. The effect left him feeling groggy and disoriented, like there was a dense fog surrounding him. Raynor couldn't see anything, even his own hand in front of his face. He stumbled blindly through the mind-haze. He heard pounding thuds close by. His vision was slowly returning; the blur of a figure was approaching him. The movement caused trails across his vision similar to a psychotropic experience.

Before he could react, a black-masked soldier stood in front of him and pointed the blaster unwaveringly in his face. It was too late to reach for the Star.

"Don't shoot! I'm not an outlaw, I'm Martian!"

The fact that he was still wearing the robes didn't help his case. As he wondered whether the Enforcers were under orders to take prisoners, shouts and a barrage of rapid fire indicated the outlaws had decided to fight back.

The Enforcer charged at Raynor but changed his trajectory to meet the immediate threat. He tossed a restraining device at Raynor's reaching hands, which wrapped them together and pulled him off the ground. His legs flailed as the device whirled with a gravimetric motor and a suspension field lifted him to the roof of the hangar and held him dangling like fruit on a tree.

CHAPTER EIGHTEEN

The last stand

Diputs became acutely aware of the ringing in his ears. Dazed and disoriented, he pushed himself up to his hands and knees, faintly remembering Lisa's shouted instruction to get down. Over the high-pitched noise, he began to make out the sound of weapons discharging. He opened his eyes wide and blinked rapidly through the haze. Slowly his vision returned. He cautiously stood up and tried to make out what was happening. Enforcers had invaded the hangar and the outlaws had taken cover behind some nearby wreckage to return fire.

"Stop shooting!" Diputs yelled out to them, but no one took any notice. He could feel the energy bursts as they whizzed over his head, crashing into the already ruined walls. He tried to stay low as he crawled towards the remaining outlaws, but pain screamed up his leg and pulsated through his whole body. He reached down with one hand and followed with his eyes to find a large piece of shrapnel sticking out of his thigh. There was nothing he could do about it in the moment. He decided he was better off leaving it where it was and tried to focus on anything but the pain.

He glanced around the hangar, but he couldn't see Serena's family or his crew. He had to move. He shifted his weight onto his other leg and pulled himself forward with his arms. The pain was excruciating but each lurch forward brought him closer to the outlaws' final stand.

He spotted Romea sitting on the ground with her back up against some wreckage. She held a blaster straight up with both hands awkwardly in front of her face. Resden was on his feet next to her, laying cover fire. Diputs got closer and saw that Romea was nursing a woman's head in her lap with the body lying away from him—blond hair spoiled with blood. The tears that he could now see streaming down Romea's cheeks made it clear that it was her mother.

"Romea!" Diputs shouted. "It's not too late. Put down your weapon and surrender. You don't have to die here like the rest of them."

She looked up at him defiantly, tears streaming down her dust-covered face. She shook her head slowly.

"This is not the will of the Divine," Diputs continued. "There is no all-powerful being that is watching over you. Only *you* can save yourself!"

"That is where you are wrong," she said gently. "In death we are free. Our souls will join the Light and become one with its love. I will join my mother and my sister once again and be happy for the rest of eternity."

"You don't *still* believe that, do you? You can't just be so willing to give up your life for some promise of a magical future after death. How do you know it's real?"

Her sad blue eyes pierced into him. "If it isn't real, then I will be dead, so it won't matter."

With a gruesome splattering of blood, Resden lost half of his face to an energy blast that skimmed across his head. He screamed in pain as his flesh sizzled from the immense heat of the energy. The stench of seared flesh filled the air, adding to the coppery taste of vaporised blood. Romea let out a desperate wail as her father's lifeless corpse fell backwards and collapsed on the broken ground. Another bolt of energy sliced through the air, burning a large hole into a piece of debris right next to Diputs' head. He pressed his chest to the ground in an attempt to stay low and searched frantically for anything nearby that he could use. A particle beam rifle lay between them, still attached to the severed arm that previously wielded it, but Diputs couldn't tell if it still had any charge left.

The firing died off and Diputs realised there was no one shooting back. He watched the Enforcers emerge from cover to explore the aftermath. Romea's breathing increase rapidly. She still held the blaster upright.

"Put it down, please!" Diputs pleaded. "It's over, everyone else is dead. Put it down and come with me." He reached his hand out as if she could pass it across the distance between them.

Multiple Enforcers closed in on them. They were clad head to toe in black panel armour, their identities concealed by an almost robotic looking mask.

Romea gently lowered her mother's head to the ground and stood. She spun around and took aim at an Enforcer. Diputs grabbed the intrusion in his leg and wrenched it out. Pain and adrenaline surged through him, jolting him to his feet. He lunged forward and crashed into her, pushing the weapon away from her intended target. It wasn't hard to dislodge her grip on the blaster, which sent it crashing to the ground, out of reach. Several Enforcers reacted and closed in with weapons drawn. One of them grabbed Diputs by his robes and dragged him back from Romea.

"We surrender," Diputs cried. "We are unarmed, we surrender, please!"

Romea pushed herself up onto her knees and looked at him bitterly. "You bastard," she uttered. He could hardly hear her speak, but he recognised the shape of the words on her lips.

"We are *not* outlaws," Diputs said, as clearly as his dry throat would allow. "We are from Mars, please don't shoot."

But as casually as one steps on an insect, the faceless man discharged his weapon and Romea's head erupted, spraying blood and brains into the air. Diputs watched Serena die for a second time. He wailed and surged to his feet once more. But he was met by the butt of a weapon against his temple. The Enforcer that wielded it spun it around, pointing the barrel directly in front of Diputs' face.

This was it. The Saturn Alliance had sent their soldiers to wipe away any sign of their indiscretion. They would cover up all traces of the fact that they had let their secret weapon slide into the hands of outlaws.

He waited for the final blow.

"Stand down," a disembodied voice ordered. "Look at his identification, this one is under the protection of the Nexus sanctions."

Diputs felt the tug of unconsciousness draw him back as his eyelids slammed shut. He drifted away, feeling sad for failing Serena, yet again.

CHAPTER NINETEEN

Debrief

Raynor floated gently in the suspension field with his arms crossed. The sounds of waves crashing against a rocky shore swelled around him. His habitat walls displayed a vast ocean from atop a cliff. He had tried to sleep, but the events of the ordeal on Luume still screamed through his mind. He couldn't get the *Altos-4* sigil out of his head. Why was it in the hangar? It was *Altos-4* technology. *Their* secrets, *their* weaponry that had gone into the construction of the Fighters. It was highly unlikely that gear like that could have been stolen from the secret laboratory, which meant that *Altos-4* must have given it to the Saturn Alliance. It made him wonder again, if they had taken the Artifact to *Altos-4*, what would they have done with it? He pulled the obscure shard out from his jacket pocket and admired its golden lustre. A *'vessel to immense power'*, was how Bainsby had described it back on *M1*. Part of a weapon so powerful that it had destroyed the homeworld.

He realised he may have to convince the others to investigate what *Altos-4* were really up to. He would definitely need to deceive Lisa, no way she would go along with this. He was still unsure how he felt about Lisa. On the one hand, she had helped him more than once, on the other, her purpose was to incriminate them. So he never knew if he could trust her. His Link flashed and chimed to alert him of the incoming message. It was Rob.

'NEED A DRINK?'

Raynor laughed to himself at the sly nudge. He floated gently to the ground and stood. He placed the Artifact back in his pocket and felt the familiar boost of energy it provided. He strode out of his Habitat, out of the lobby and towards Rob's lab.

The metal stool grated against the floor as he dragged it out from the tall wooden benchtop. Rob placed a small glass on the table and spilled golden liquid into it from a transparent bottle. Raynor knocked it back, feeling the warmth burn its way down his throat and into his stomach. Rob wasted no time refilling the empty glass the moment it landed. The second one went down just as smoothly.

"You want to talk about it?" Rob prodded.

Raynor took a deep breath. He looked at his hands, now clean from the molecular shower in his Habitat. "Are we any different from them?"

"What do you mean? The outlaws?"

"Yes."

"We do what we have to. To survive."

"So do they," Raynor said. He ran a hand through his messy hair. "Sure, they believe a whole lot of stupidity to try and justify their actions, but in the end, most of them are just trying to fight for their freedom from the Colonies."

"No, they are trying to destroy the Colonies. They could run away and live further out, not bother us, but—"

"Do you really think we would just let them be? The UAE was put together to fight them."

"To *defend* against them. Don't confuse the individual with the cause. So you met some of them, got to know that they are real people with real feelings and real lives. You know better than to empathise with the enemy. Where's your soldier's conditioning?"

"When did you start regurgitating colonial propaganda like a model citizen? You weren't there. You have no idea what happened."

"Just because the Colonies are wrong, it doesn't make the outlaws right," Rob said. "You can't defy a cause without defying the people who implement and enforce it. Yes, it is sad that some people died, but they died because of what they were doing, not because of us."

What surprised Raynor more, was that he never normally let himself get emotionally involved. Yet he couldn't get the image of Romea's innocent eyes and her sharp wit out of his mind. The Enforcers had spared no one, apart from those of the *Galaxy* crew, who all had been granted diplomatic protection. Outlaws had no value and thus, deserved no protection, no rights, beyond rehabilitation.

Before Raynor even knew where to begin, the door vanished, permitting Diputs to the hideaway. Magically, a glass was waiting for him and Rob's quick fingers resealed the bottle of liquor after pouring them all a drink. Diputs looked sullen as he made his way over to the bar. Rob and Raynor watched silently as he perched on a stool, drained his glass and looked up at them.

"Well, what are you bloody looking at?"

Raynor ventured a question. "Are you..."

"Alright?" Diputs finished. "Of course not. What do you think? I failed. *Again.* And this time, a lot of people paid the price."

Rob jumped in first. "You can't blame yourself for any of this. You know that, right?"

"Why not? If it wasn't for me, Serena wouldn't be dead, and neither would her family. How can I *not* blame myself for this? And I might have missed my chance to find out about my parents."

"Your parents?"

"Evon knew my parents, apparently. But now, I will never know if that was true or not."

"That sounds like he just made it up. He was just trying to control you," Raynor said. "Trust me, I know what these control-freak types are like."

"No," Diputs said. "He knew my real name, Raynor. And now I will never know more, because he didn't make it out alive."

"At least *we* made it out alive," Jake added, almost cheerfully.

They all jumped in fright.

"Jake! You just about scared me half to death," Diputs said.

"Why does no one tell me when you are all drinking?"

"You know when we are drinking," Rob chuckled as he spoke. He slapped the boy on the back and poured him a glass.

"Thanks," Jake said as he lifted the glass to his lips. "But a heads up would be nice. I didn't think you would be doing this, you know, with Lisa still around."

Raynor laughed. "Why would she make any difference?"

"You do know, she won't be fooled forever," Jake started. "When we go for drinks, she's going to wonder where we all are. All it would take, is for her to try and find us. What if she did that right now? She'd take one look at us with a prohibited substance and have our asses—"

"She won't have anything. You think she doesn't know already? She hasn't made a big deal about it because she wants more shit on us. We'd get a slap on the wrists for this, at most. She wants us to go down, just like Reen."

"Or maybe she just likes flirting with you," Jake said jokingly.

Raynor smacked him on the back of the head.

Jake rubbed the point of impact. "Ow, what was that for?"

They all went quiet as they returned to their drinking and Rob filled them up for another round. Raynor had slowed to sipping at his drink.

"I noticed something in the hangar," Raynor said. "The tech that they used to build those Fighters. There's no way a bunch of simple outlaws managed to design and build such advanced machines on their own. They had help... from *Altos-4*."

"That's not possible," Rob exclaimed. "Why on Mars would they have anything to do with this?"

"I don't know why, but they did. I saw the *Altos-4* crates. The technology must have come from there. There's no doubt about it," Raynor countered.

"Perhaps someone stole it?" Rob said.

"That's even harder to believe. Very few people know it exists. Which makes me wonder if there is some conspiracy to destabilise the Nexus? Remember, we were originally ordered to take the Artifact to *Altos-4*," Raynor said. "What would they want with the Artifact? They are definitely up to *something*. We need to investigate."

"Why do I feel like we are just being used as pawns here?" Diputs said.

Raynor looked around at them conspiratorially. "I say we should pay them a visit. I say we find out what is really going on here."

Rob was astonished. "We can't do that! What do you think we are going to say to them when we get there? *'oh hi fella's, we're just here to take a look around and see if anything suspicious is going on?'*, It's *Altos-fucking-four*! It's not even supposed to exist!"

"So what?" Diputs challenged. "Are we supposed to just go along with this? Pretend none of it ever happened? How do we even know we are on the right side here?"

Diputs looked around at them, determination in his eyes. "I mean look, I'm not saying that I believe in any of that *Light of the Divine* garbage. But maybe they are right to challenge our way of life under the corrupt leadership of the Colonies. I mean, let's not forget, *we* aren't exactly model citizens. We break the rules at every turn because we think… no, we *know* that we know better."

"I suppose you've got a point," Rob said. "If we are going to go all out, then I've got a few things that I wouldn't mind taking a look at on the *Altos-4* database."

"Then it's settled," Raynor said as he raised his glass. "To *Altos-4.*"

CHAPTER TWENTY

Interrogation

Evon opened his eyes slowly and once again became aware of his surroundings. The pain had been too much, and he had lost consciousness. The energy barriers of his cell glowed blue, giving off the only real light in the room. He was still strapped to the bench and the cell reeked of blood. His blood. He looked down to assess the damage. His right foot had been severed, just above the ankle. He could still feel it though. His mind played tricks on him as he tried to rotate his phantom limb.

His torturer stood in the far corner of the cell in a white Lunar Colony uniform, splattered with blood. The man who wore it was rugged and unshaven. Scars criss-crossed his face, perhaps signs that he had once been in the same position—a victim to torture and colonial inquisition. The device his tormentor carried over glowed red with heat. He looked away as the device was jammed into the end of his stump to cauterize the wound. Evon screamed as the agony forced its way through his nervous system. He called out to a God he knew would not answer him.

The torturer spoke in a low and even voice. "Do you feel like talking now?"

"You may as well kill me," Evon yelled through the pain.

"Why would I do that? Do you think I am going to let you off that easily?" The man wiped the blood from his hands. "We have work to do, you and I."

"I'll never help you."

"Oh! I like it when they play hard to get!"

Something on the torturer's coat captured Evon's attention. A small silver emblem on the white collar. "That symbol, do you even know what that is?" Evon asked.

The torturer looked down and then touched it.

"That's strange. Most people are programmed not to notice this symbol. It's nothing of any importance to this situation. Why?"

"I have seen it before, a similar design. It is part of a mural of Sol on the floor of one of the great cathedrals on Triton. It represents the Divine Light, our God."

The torturer scoffed. "You people...you have to personify everything. Yes, there are secrets that we can learn from our sun. It gives us life, but by itself does not sustain us. We have the power, we *are* the light, we determine the course of humanity."

"And yet, Sol can take it all away from us. It could engulf all life and we would be powerless to stop it."

"Perhaps."

The instruments rattled as he dropped the tool on the tray.

"Why are you doing this?" Evon groaned, stalling for more time.

"You have this around the wrong way, friend. I ask the questions and you answer them. If you don't feel like talking, then I remove some more body parts. But rest assured that this doesn't end with your death. Oh no. This ends with you becoming my new little tool."

Evon saw a glint of enjoyment in the man's eyes as he picked up the metal saw blade. The blunt metal teeth were still filthy from chewing away at his other leg. It had intentionally not been a clean cut and the tool was already worn and broken from the effort. The blade kissed his left leg, this time above the knee. Evon winced as his brain prepared him for another round of excruciating agony. He found himself praying silently. He didn't expect anything to happen, but the ritual of the words rushing through his brain distracted him from the horror about to unfold.

Suddenly, he felt a moment of clarity. Who was he trying to protect, and why? His family back on the icy moon of Triton flashed through his thoughts. Would they be affected if he gave in now? His followers were all dead and his superiors… this was all their fault anyway. Them, and the child of the late Jane and Ceptis Baulkham—the so-called prophesied leader of the free people.

If he helped the Colonies, then at least he may have his revenge.

"I'll do it!" Evon screamed. "I'll tell you everything. I'll help you. I know who *he* is. The man who will change everything."

BOOK FOUR

CONNIVANCE

When Raynor receives a call for help from his dispatch supervisor, he convinces the rest of the crew to walk into an obvious trap in order to gain access to a wealth of information kept in the DataCore of the esoteric *Altos-4*. Once inside, they find more than just encrypted secrets. Inhuman threats lurking in the darkness twist their rescue and recovery mission into a fight for their lives.

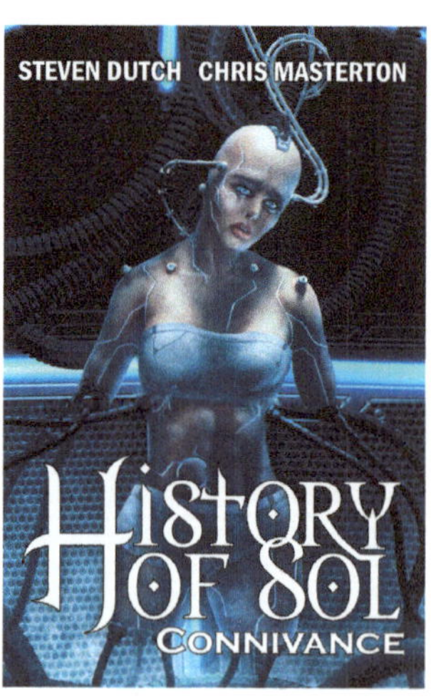

About The Author

Chris Masterton

Chris is a space nerd, tech enthusiast, and sci-fi author. He enjoys exploring themes such as the future of humanity, artificial intelligence, and the impact technology has on society. Chris has a background in software and graphic design.

Connect with Chris:

- www.chrism.au

- goodreads.com/chrismasterton

About The Author

Steven Dutch

 Steven Dutch was born in Auckland, New Zealand but grew up in Sydney, Australia. He would consider himself a foodie, and enjoys most cultures' foods. He works a day job as a Cyber Security Service Delivery Manager and enjoys everything scientific and technological, which bleeds over into his writing often. He has always been fascinated by science fiction and magic, thinking there is a fine line between the two and enjoys writing stories meshing and melding the two together. He has been writing for over 12 years and has completed several writing seminars and courses.

Connect with Steven:

- goodreads.com/stevendutch

History of Sol

H istory of Sol is an action/adventure sci-fi novella series set in the distant future.

Find out about the latest releases and where you can meet the authors using our social media links:

- historyofsol.com

- facebook.com/history.of.sol

- instagram.com/historyofsol

- twitter.com/historyofsol

Glossary

- **Enforcers:** Responsible for maintaining law and order

- **Foreseer:** Manages and assigns roles based on the needs of their Colony

- **Observer:** Spy/Intelligence gatherer

- **Peacekeeper:** The highest level of Nexus administration

- **Datafile:** An automated file system that gathers and sorts all information in the Nexus

- **Data Crystal:** A small quartz disk that serves as a mobile data storage device

- **Habitat:** A self-contained living area on smaller spacecraft

- **Interface:** Computer

- **Krontonium:** A rare element used to power the Star

- **Link:** Communication device / Mobile personal interface

- **Mitron:** Microscopic unit of measurement

- **Millitrons:** Tiny unit of measurement

- **Centron:** Small unit of measurement

- **Metron:** Medium unit of measurement

- **Kiltron:** Large unit of measurement

- **Nexus:**

- **a) name -** The governing body uniting all of the colonies under the 'Nexus Treaty'

- **b) technology -** A colony-wide shared communication and data system

- **Node:** A subsystem component of a Nexus or Datafile

- **Organix:** Liquid sustenance

- **Outlaw:** A general term used to denote people without Value

- **Robotoid:** A small self-mobilised robot

- **Rotation:** The time it takes for Mars to complete one rotation around its axis

- **Sub-Cycle:** 1/24th of a Cycle

- **Cycle:** The orbital period of Mars to pass once around Sol

- **Tectanium:** A super-strong metal derived from Titanium and enhanced with nano-tech

- **The Artifact:** A small shard of unknown material and origin

- **The Star:** A quantum state transference with a conduit of antimatter resonance (converts matter into light for brief periods of time)

- **The Terranean Expanse:** An asteroid belt between Lunar and Venus

- **Theridium Alpha:** A rare form of radioactive material found in the Kuiper belt

- **Unity:** A formal partnership between two or more people

- **Value:** Economic recognition based on contribution to a colony